DATE DUE

THE BEST IDEAS IN THE WORLD ARE FREE

Undercurrent

Undercurrent

Bill Pronzini

Random House: New York

Copyright © 1973 by BILL PRONZINI

All rights reserved under International
and Pan-American Copyright Conventions.
Published in the United States by Random House, Inc., New York
and simultaneously in Canada
by Random House of Canada Limited, Toronto.

Library of Congress Cataloging in Publication Data
Pronzini, Bill.
Undercurrent.

I. Title.
PZ4.P9653Un [PS3566.R67]   813'.5'4   73–1931
ISBN 0–394–48265–4

Manufactured in the United States of America
9 8 7 6 5 4 3 2
First Edition

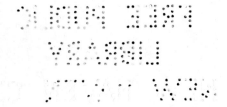

This One Is for (and for the Memory of):

Francis K. Allan   Lester Dent
W. T. Ballard   William Campbell Gault
Fredric Brown   G. T. Fleming-Roberts
John K. Butler   John D. MacDonald
Frederick C. Davis   Robert Martin
Norbert Davis   Talmage Powell
Robert C. Dennis   Robert Turner
Cornell Woolrich

And All the Thousands of Other Writers
Who Made the Pulps Such a Joy—Yesterday and Today

Undercurrent

One

It was one of those jobs you take on when things are very lean. You want to turn it down—it's an old story, and a sordid one, and a sad one—but you know you can't afford to. The rent falls due in a few days and the savings account is all but depleted; you haven't worked in almost three weeks, and the boredom and the emptiness are beginning to take their toll. So you look into tear-filmed gray eyes, and you sigh, and you say yes . . .

Judith Paige was the kind of girl they used to call "sweet" and "wholesome" without sniggering about it. In her middle twenties, maybe, she had a shy, quiet way of moving and of talking that put you on her side the minute you saw her. She was innocence with character, sugar with a little spice; if you were my age, and a bachelor too, she made you think about and ache a little for the daughter you never had, the love you never had that could have conceived someone like her.

She had a slender, supple body, outfitted in a lace-bodiced white blouse and one of those fold-over suede skirts that button at the side and are supposed to be popular in Europe these days. Over narrow shoulders was a suede jacket, of the same beige color as the skirt; the two did not quite match, however, and so I knew that she was something less than monetarily well-set-up. But I also knew that she cared, that she was willing to make an effort in her own behalf. Too many of them have long since stopped caring, for too many reasons.

You could not really call her beautiful, but she had that aura of youth and sweetness that was like a magnetic attraction. And pale-blond hair, cropped short on a small round head; those glistening gray eyes, like misty circles in a window through which you can see the glow and warmth of a soft inner fire; a small, expressive mouth and a nose that was hardly even there. When she smiled, even forcing it as she did, it was like being caressed by a little girl; and when she cried, it was like hearing that same little girl lamenting the death of a puppy. I felt uncomfortable with her from the moment she stepped into my office, because she stirred my emotions, and the last thing I needed just then was to have my emotions stirred.

She sat nervously in the chair across my desk, and looked at the desk and at the window and at the floor as she told her story in a soft voice filled with embarrassment. Until the previous year she had lived in a small town in Idaho; at that time she had decided to move to San Francisco to "search for some meaning in life"—which meant, of course, that she had come looking for a husband. The Idaho town, although she did not say it, had obviously and not surprisingly failed to yield any man worthy of her. The way it looked, so had San Francisco.

But she had found one here, a guy named Walter Paige. They had been married three months now, and it was something far less than the idyllic union she had expected. It was not that Paige abused her in any way, or was a drinker or a gambler— like that; it was simply that in the past five weeks he had taken to leaving her alone on the weekends. He told her it was business—he worked for some industrial supply house—and when she pressed him for details, he grew reticent. He was working on a couple of large prospects, he said, that would set them both up nicely in the future.

She figured he was working on another woman.

Like I said, an old story, and a sordid one, and a sad one.

She wanted me to follow him for a few days, to either confirm or deny her suspicions. That was all. You don't need to prove adultery, or much of anything else, to obtain a divorce in California these days, so I would not be required to testify in any civil proceedings. It was just that she had to know, one way or the other—the tears starting then—and if she was right, she wanted to dissolve the marriage and maybe go back to Idaho, she just didn't know at this point. She had a little money saved and she could pay my standard rates, and she had heard that I was honest and capable and that I would not take advantage of her in any way . . .

I sat there behind my desk, feeling old and tired and cynical. It was a nice day outside, as days in San Francisco go, and I had the window open a little. The breeze off the bay was cool and fresh on the back of my neck. Late April sunshine put a liquid gold veneer across one corner of the desk. Nice spring day, all right. A day for sailing languidly on the bay, or taking in a base-ball game at Candlestick, or driving through fragrant woods and fields. A day for looking at somebody else's soiled linen, laid out to air in your office.

I got a cigarette out of the pack on the frayed blotter and lighted it and blew smoke at the beam of sunlight. It drifted and curled in the soft glow, like half-remembered dreams in the light of dawn. I looked away from there and put my eyes on Judith Paige and thought that she was too young and too nice to have the kind of problem that would bring her to a man in my profes-sion. She should have been happy and carefree, her laughter should have rung loud and clear in the sunshine. But then, prag-matically, there were things I could not know about. She might

5

have been frigid, or a poor cook and a lousy housekeeper, or unable to adapt to living with a man. She might have picked a guy who was a chaser by nature, a bastard by nature. Or she might only be jumping at shadows. It would be nice if that was the way it turned out—only it seldom does, not nearly often enough to make you optimistic about it.

I took one of the contract forms out of the bottom drawer and slid it over for her to examine. When she had, I drew it back and filled it out accordingly; her answers to my questions were simple and direct. I gave the contract over to her again for her signature, and then I said, "All right, Mrs. Paige. What can you tell me about these weekend trips of your husband's?"

"Not . . . very much, I'm afraid," looking at the single metal file cabinet with the hot plate and the coffee pot resting on its top.

"Have you any idea at all where he goes?"

"Only that it doesn't seem to be in this immediate area."

"What makes you say that?"

"Well, I checked the . . . mileage thing on the car last week," she said. "Before Walter left and after he came back. There was more than two hundred miles' difference in the two figures."

"I see. Is there anything else?"

"No. No, nothing."

"He hasn't given you any hint?"

"No. Whenever I ask, he smiles and tells me it's a very private sort of business deal and he's not supposed to talk to anyone about it, even his wife."

I worked on my cigarette and pretended to examine the contract form. "I don't mean to be blunt, Mrs. Paige, but do you have any tangible reason for your suspicions?"

Her eyes touched me briefly, and then flicked away again. "Tangible reason?"

I knew the words would sound harsh and cruel before I said

6

them, but I said them anyway. "Letters, lipstick marks, unexplained items or photographs of any kind?"

She seemed to shudder slightly and a faint pink suffused the silken whiteness of her cheeks. "No," she said in a small, soft voice. "Nothing like that. It's just that Walter . . . isn't . . . well, he isn't very . . . attentive to me after he . . . For the first day or two after he returns, he . . ." She could not get the rest of it out. Her eyes were on her hands now, watching the long and slender fingers pluck nervously at the buttons on her suede jacket.

I felt like a kind of mental voyeur, and I got off that tack for both our sakes. I said, "Your husband's gone away each of the past four Saturdays, is that right?"

"Yes, that's right."

"Do you know for certain he'll go again tomorrow?"

"Oh yes," she said. "He told me last night. He said he would be staying until late Monday this time, but not . . . not why."

"Was that when you decided to come to me?"

Her throat worked. "Yes."

"What time does he usually leave?"

"Around nine or so."

"And when has he been coming back?"

"Late Sunday afternoon."

"Any particular time?"

"No. Between five and eight, about."

"Does he drive?"

"Yes."

"What kind of car?"

"A dark-blue Cutlass."

"Do you know the license number?"

"Well, I wrote that down. I thought you'd need to have it." She opened a suede purse and looked at a piece of paper from inside. "It's TTD-six-seven-nine."

I wrote the number on the contract margin. I could not think of anything more to ask her. What was there to ask in a case like this? They give you the barest details, because that's all they know themselves; you get an idea of what time he leaves her, and then you go out to where they live and camp on the street and follow him until you're sure one way or the other. Usually you don't have to drive more than ten miles; maybe I would have to drive two hundred, and maybe I would not have to. If Paige had another woman, she could live right here in San Francisco, and they could have gone to the beach last weekend to play their games—or to the mountains or any damned place at all. It had always seemed rather pointless to me that they would go *anywhere,* even though they sometimes do; the beds in San Francisco motels or apartments are no different from those at the beach or in the mountains.

I said, "Well, I guess that's about all I'll need, Mrs. Paige. I'll be on the job early in the morning. Try to act natural tonight and tomorrow—and don't check out the door or window for me before he leaves."

She nodded once, convulsively, and her hands were restless on the suede bag. "You won't let him know you're following him, will you? I mean, if I'm wrong and Walter is just . . . working, I wouldn't want him to know what I've done . . ."

"I'll be as careful as I can."

"Thank you," she said, and her lower lip trembled slightly. There were more tears building in her eyes, but she would not let them get out until she was alone; they were the kind of tears a woman cries only when she is alone. "Will you call me as soon as you find out anything?"

"Right away."

"Shall I give you a check now?"

"I can bill you."

"Well, I'd like to give you something."

"All right."

"Twenty-five dollars?"

"That would be fine, Mrs. Paige."

I looked away while she made out the check. Through the window I could see the rising spans of the Bay Bridge in the distance. Somewhere out there, on the bay itself, a ship's whistle sounded. I thought: Freighter going out, down to Panama, maybe, or off to the Far East. God, how nice it must be out there on the sea! Wind and spray washing over you, washing you clean. You can't get clean in the city; there's too much dirt, tangible and intangible, literal and figurative . . .

She put the check on my blotter, and I got it into the center drawer without looking at it. Then I stood up and she stood up, and there was nothing for either of us to say in the way of parting. I went with her to the door, and held it for her, and she gave me her shy, wistful little smile and went out hugging the suede jacket tightly around her, as if she were very cold.

When she was gone, I closed the door and went back to my desk and opened the center drawer and looked at her check lying within. Twenty-five dollars advance. Seventy-five total, plus expenses, if the job lasted just the one day. Seventy-five bucks to become a part of the private life and private emotions of a nice young girl. How does it make you feel, guy? Like a gigolo, maybe? Like a goddamned heel?

I closed the drawer again and got my hat and my lightweight overcoat from the office alcove and locked the door behind me and went out into the sunshine. It seemed faintly gray somehow, even though the sky was cloudless, and there was no warmth in it. The young girls in their spring fashions reminded me of Judith Paige, and there was no warmth in that either.

Two

I left my flat in Pacific Heights at seven-fifteen the following morning, and drove out to the address Judith Paige had given me—on Sussex Street, in Glen Park. It was one of those borderline neighborhoods that never seem to be able to make up their minds which way to go. The streets ran in twisting confusion—climbing sharply, dropping sharply, dead-ending with no warning at all—and on each of them you saw fairly nice, if old, middle-class homes, and shabby unpainted tenements, and new low-rent apartment buildings, and old low-rent duplexes. The business district, off Monterey Boulevard, was comprised of grim-visaged shops and buildings that gave you the odd feeling of having regressed thirty or forty years into the dim, Depression past.

The Paiges lived in one of the apartment dwellings on upper Sussex—a two-story, four-unit thing with an ocher-colored plaster façade and tiny balconies railed in black iron. On the street in front, parked facing downhill, was a dark-blue Cutlass with the license number TTD-679. I drove up to the top of Sussex, turned around in somebody's driveway, and came down to park on the upper edge of a convex hook in the street, sixty yards or so above the Cutlass. I could see the entrance to the apartment building from there as well. My watch said that it was seven-fifty.

I got my cigarettes out and looked at them and put them away again. My chest felt tight and hot, and I had coughed up a wad of gray-flecked phlegm over my breakfast coffee. Bronchial trouble, created and nurtured by the consumption of too many cigarettes—or maybe it was the other thing, the dark thing you don't like to think about. No. Bronchial trouble, that's all it was. What was the point in wasting money on a doctor to confirm it? Bronchial trouble. Sure.

The simple truth is, you don't want to know.

The simple truth is, you're afraid to find out.

So the hell with it.

A guy and his family came out of a stucco-fronted house on my side of the street, carrying picnic baskets, and got into a vintage Ford and drove off down the hill. The front door banged in the house next door to that one, and a woman with ankles like a heron's legs and a body as thin as a wafer began hunting for her morning paper; she found it after a while, used it to scratch herself in an intimate place, and shuffled back inside again. An elderly lady with too much rouge on her cheeks struggled up the hill with a lean poodle on a red leash; the poodle made a pass for my right front tire, and the elderly lady jerked him away, smiling at me in a self-consciously apologetic way. When I glanced up into my rear-view mirror a moment later, the poodle was washing off the right front tire on the car parked behind mine, while she looked on; that car was empty. Three kids came flying down the opposite sidewalk on roller skates, laughing and shouting. One of them took a header down by the Cutlass—a fat kid in baggy pants—and rolled over in the gutter and began to cry; the other two sailed on down the hill, taunting over their shoulders, and the fat one sat there in the gutter and watched them forlornly with the tears running down his cheeks. Then he got up and took off his skates and began to trudge slowly up the hill. I was sorry for him, because I knew, a little, how he felt.

Eight-fifteen.

There had been a high, early-morning fog, but it was lifting off now and the sky was a faded indigo to the east. Sunlight, the universal cleanser, washed the street and the houses in pale gold, and the neighborhood looked a little nicer, a little friendlier, a little more hopeful. The smell of spring was thick and fresh in the air.

Across the street a woman with reddish-gold hair that shone like distant fire came out of her house and went into a side garden; she carried a trowel and a pair of gardening gloves. For a brief instant the flaming hair reminded me of Cheryl Rosmond. I looked away and got out my cigarettes and lit one—the hell with my chest.

Cheryl Rosmond. A memory now—still vivid, still immediate, but a memory nonetheless. She was something that might have been for me, something that should have been, something which now could never be. The attraction, the rapport, we had had, had died before it had really lived—the result of a tragedy which neither of us could have foreseen in the beginning, and which, bitterly, neither of us could have prevented even if we had.

It had died because I had unmasked her brother—her only living relative, the one person she loved more than anything in this world—as a cold-blooded murderer, and because I had been an integral part of the reason for his ultimate suicide by hanging.

What can you say to a woman after something like that? How can you bridge the sudden chasm between you? The answers are painfully simple: there is nothing you can say, there is no way to span the chasm. You cannot bring her brother back to life, and undo his wrongs, and you cannot bring back to life the spark that had begun between you and her; both are dead, both are gone. And the fact that Doug Rosmond had addressed his suicide note to me, and begged me to take care of his sister and to love her and to help her, only made the situation that much more untenable; he would always be between us, the ghost of him and of his crimes, even if our relationship could have somehow continued. Cheryl knew that, and I knew it, and there was simply nothing more for either of us.

But I tried. You have to try. I saw her, I called her—and it was useless, so damned futile because all the while you *know* it's futile. The papers made a thing out of the case—there was no way to keep it out of the papers—and that had made it unbearable for Cheryl in San Francisco; she had given up her house on Vicente and given up her job and her few friends and moved back to Truckee, where she had grown up but where she had no family and she was as alone as I. I had written her four times since then, and she had answered each letter politely but with no encouragement, and then I had stopped writing and stopped myself three times from getting into my car and driving up to the Sierras to see her again, because you can only try for so long before you have to admit the absolute finality of it, the impossibility of resurrection. So now it was over; it was buried along with Doug Rosmond.

I had made a promise to myself then that I would no longer become involved, that involvement brought pain more acute than that of simple loneliness. It had been a rough six months for me, because before Cheryl there had been a woman named Erika, who had walked out of my life for a much different if no less painful reason, and I did not think I could endure another bittersweet love affair—now or ever again. I was too old, too tired, too sensitive. It was better to be a loner, to be alone, to be objective; the pleasures were few, but they were good and simple ones, and the less complications there were, the more peaceful life was.

I finished the cigarette and threw the butt out the window and watched the languid breeze roll it down the hill toward the silently waiting Cutlass. Almost nine now. Come on, Paige, let's get the show on the road, let's get your ass in gear. If you're screwing around on a girl like Judith, you son of a bitch, you're the biggest damned fool who ever walked the earth. Don't you see what you've got there? Don't you know how fortunate you are? Don't you know there are those who would give their eyes for the love of a woman like that?

Another five minutes went by, darkly. I felt nervous and irritable with the waiting; I wished I had not seen the woman with the reddish-gold hair, and I wished that Judith Paige had not come into my office the day before. I could have called Eberhardt—my best friend for better than twenty-five years, the youthfully idealistic days at the Police Academy and on the San Francisco cops, where he was currently a Lieutenant of Detectives—and have talked him into going fishing up at Black Point. We could have sat in a skiff and drunk beer in the warm spring sunshine and enjoyed life a little, the simple pleasures . . .

The entrance door to the apartment building opened, and a lean, sinuous guy carrying an overnight bag and wearing a sports coat over a thin brown turtleneck came out briskly. He had one of these sharp-featured faces that you could call handsome if you liked the type, and curly black hair and long barlike sideburns. He walked quickly to the Cutlass, unlocked the driver's door, and slid in under the wheel.

I waited until he was half a block down the hill before I started my car and pulled out after him. Once we got off Sussex, there was just enough traffic so that I could stay fairly close—and he led me directly to the Southern Freeway entrance on Monterey Boulevard. I gave him a long lead out on the freeway, and then closed the gap a little as we neared the arteries branching into the James Lick north and south, and into 280 leading down to Third Street; I half expected him to make the

14

swing north, into San Francisco proper, but he cut over to the right instead and got onto James Lick southbound. If there was another woman, she did not apparently live in the city.

Paige held his speed down in the moderately heavy traffic, driving leisurely, and I had no trouble keeping him in sight. If you put other cars between yourself and your subject, and use a lane opposite to his, maintaining a tail on the freeway is no real problem—as long as the subject does not expect to be followed in the first place. Paige seemed to have no suspicions whatsoever.

We went down the length of the peninsula on 101, leaving the bay and its crisp breezes behind. We left San Jose behind too—and then Gilroy and Watsonville—and it began to look as if the two-hundred-odd miles Paige had driven the previous weekend meant something after all. The further south we traveled, the warmer it got to be. We passed through the agricultural belt, the fields of lettuce and artichokes—Steinbeck country; and a few miles outside of Salinas, Paige finally quit 101 on State 156 leading west toward the ocean. Just below Castroville, 156 joins Highway 1, and when we got there, Paige swung south again along the coast.

Highway 1 was two-lane and had considerably less traffic; I dropped further back with a car between the Cutlass and me. Artichoke fields stretched away on both sides of the road for a while, but when we approached Fort Ord—the Army's West Coast training camp—the landscape changed to seaward and became a series of rolling sand dunes topped with tule grass, like an endless string of human heads with all the features and most of the hair erased by the sea winds. The buildings of Fort Ord came and went, as did the town of Seaside, and pretty soon we were in more of Steinbeck country—the city of Monterey.

We came down off a steep hill on the southern outskirts, and through thickly grown Monterey cypress and pine I had my first glimpse of the Pacific, and of the small inlet of Cypress Bay;

the water was blue-green and sun-jeweled, dotted with sailboats and pleasure craft. A little further along, there was a turnoff for the village of Cypress Bay; Paige took the exit, and we began to descend along a wood-lined concourse toward the center of the hamlet.

Cypress Bay was a haven for artists and writers—and for sightseers and vacationers and college students and hippies and the more sedate among the swingers. Art galleries and workshops, more than a hundred souvenir shops, quaint French and seafood restaurants, and dozens of motels, hotels, and inns comprised the bulk of its buildings; and there were pastoral streets and curving little alleys to complete the illusion of a vanished and cherished rusticity. You would find no billboards, few street signs, few street lights; the city fathers maintained and protected the illusion with strict building codes and rigid laws. The architecture was a mixture of traditional Old Spanish; Monterey adobe, which utilized waterproof adobe bricks and redwood shakes and hewn local timbers; log-cabin style, with heavy emphasis on pioneer simplicity; and saccharine Hansel and Gretel doll houses, popular in the twenties, that featured whimsical windows, chimneys, gambrels, and gabled roofs. You had to go some distance outside the village proper to find anything of a modern design.

Paige took me through the middle of Cypress Bay on Grove Avenue—a two-lane street divided in the middle by shrubbery, lined with souvenir shops and spanned at intervals by banners proclaiming: *Sentinel Hill Professional Golf Classic · Thursday, May 4, Through Sunday, May 7 · Qualifying Monday, May 1.* Sentinel Hill, like its more famous neighbor Pebble Beach, was located on the peninsula not far from Cypress Bay; and the annual pro tournament there, like the ones at Pebble, always brought in a heavy stream of tourists and camp followers. From the packed sidewalks, it appeared as if most of them had arrived early.

16

At the foot of Grove was a wide thoroughfare called Ocean Boulevard, which ran in a parallel curve to the harbor. Across it was a large, thickly shaded park, a municipal pier where you could hire a charter boat for salmon trolling or deep-sea fishing, and a public beach that curved in a white-powder crescent around the inlet. Cypress Bay had a little something for everyone; I wondered sourly what it had for Walter Paige.

Paige made a left turn on Ocean and drove a fifth of a mile; there, beachfront, was a motel that you might have mistaken for a series of private beach cottages if you had glanced at them in a cursory way. The only sign was a small, neat, bucolic one with letters fashioned out of strips of bark; it said: *The Beachwood.*

Paige took the Cutlass onto a white-gravel drive and stopped in front of a log-cabin-style building in the middle of the grounds; the drive formed a small inner square, servicing each of the cottages in their squared-off, extended U arrangement. I stopped on Ocean Boulevard and watched Paige get out and enter the motel office.

This looked like the end of the line—for now, anyway. But I was not going in until I made certain. So I sat there, waiting, and looked at the cottages. They were as neat and rustic as the sign, as the rest of Cypress Bay. Pines filled the grounds—and roses and lilac bushes—and each cottage was separated from its neighbor by a high Monterey cypress hedge. Those cottages at the rear of the grounds had their backsides to the sea and to what looked like a private beach; the others, which formed the shortened arms of the U, seemed to have lush rear gardens bounded by more of the cypress hedges. A little something for everyone here, too—in keeping with the community image. But the Beachwood was not a place for the flotsam and jetsam that washed into Cypress Bay in the spring and summer months— and that made me wonder a little. It seemed well out of Paige's range, judging from his San Francisco address, but then, it could be that he was not paying for the accommodations.

Paige reappeared after a couple of minutes and got into the Cutlass again and drove it over to one of the cottages offering a rear view of the sea, parking under a kind of shake-roofed porte-cochere attached to the side wall. Then he got out with his overnight bag and used a key on the front door.

I sat there for ten minutes, but he did not come out again. I started my car and entered the white-gravel drive and parked in approximately the same spot as Paige had originally. When I stepped out, I could see that the number of his cottage was 9. I went into the office, and it was a dark, well-appointed room with a counter at one end and unvarnished redwood walls. A bell over the door announced my entrance, and a guy dressed in a gray business suit appeared through a doorway behind the counter and smiled at me in a professional way. He was a couple of years younger than my forty-seven, with a round, pink, complacent face and a mouth that was red enough to have been made up with lip rouge. A small rectangular card pinned to the breast pocket of his suit coat said that he was Mr. Orchard.

"Yes, sir?" He had a rich, masculine voice that belied the fruity appearance of his lips. "May I help you?"

I told him I wanted a sea-view cottage—8, 9, or 10, if any of those were available. Apologetically: they were not; in fact, all of the rear cottages were occupied at the moment. I asked him what he had with southern exposure, and he said that both 6 and 7 were free.

"May I see one before I register?"

"Certainly, sir." He took a couple of keys off a slotted wall-board to one side and led me out and across the grounds to Number 6. One room, with bath; good-sized, containing a double bed and naugehyde chairs and a desk and redwood walls and a beamed ceiling—and a television set in one corner that spoiled the entire effect. The rear wall, behind tasteful gold monk's-cloth drapes, was of glass, with a sliding glass door; it looked out onto the private rear garden, but I was more interested in

18

the view from the front window. I pulled bamboo blinds aside and looked over at Number 9. The angle was pretty good, if a little further away than I would have liked; I could see the front door clearly.

"It looks okay," I said to Orchard. "How much per day?"

"Twenty-five dollars, sir."

"Well, that's fine," I told him, even though it wasn't. "I'll only be here tonight, I think."

We went back to the office and I filled in the registration form and paid Orchard in advance and took my car over to the porte-cochere for Number 6. Inside, I drew one of the naugehyde chairs up to the window; then I pulled the blinds halfway up and sat down in the chair with my cigarettes and my thoughts to wait for something to happen.

Three

Nothing happened until a quarter to one, and then it was not much.

The boredom of waiting had led to too many cigarettes, and the cigarettes had led to a thin pulsing headache and a deepening of the tightness in my chest. I began to cough a little—dry, sharp sounds like the barking of a very old hound. I stood up and paced back and forth in front of the window to ease cramped muscles, holding a handkerchief over my mouth to catch the phlegm, not looking at the handkerchief, not thinking about the phlegm. I wished to Christ this other woman would come, so I could call Judith Paige and confirm her fears and listen to her cry; they always cry when you tell them, even though they expect the worst. Then I could go home and drink a couple of bottles of beer and try to forget the entire damned thing. Or I wished that Paige would do something to alleviate suspicion completely, to restore some of my tenuous faith in the basic goodness of man; my telephone call, and Judith Paige's tears, would have different meanings then, and those beers would taste better and my apartment would be a little less lonely tonight.

My throat felt dry, and I went into the bathroom and drank a glass of water. When I returned to the window, Paige was several steps from the front door of his cottage, walking without haste along the white-gravel drive toward Ocean Boulevard.

I watched him from the window until he had passed the motel office, and then I opened my door and stepped out into the warm, salt-fragrant afternoon. I came around a couple of conifers in time to see Paige turn left on the boulevard and begin to make his way toward the village proper. He could not be going far, I thought, if he was walking and not driving. Maybe this was it—something, anyway, to give me an idea of which way this thing was going to go.

I gave him a good fifty yards, and followed him on the same side of the boulevard. The sidewalks were filled with humanity, and their bright faces reflected the joy of problem-free moments and a day abundant in the sweet breath of early spring; I felt a little like an alien among them.

Paige went along the edge of the white beach and entered the verdurous park I had seen earlier. Picnickers and chess players, relaxers and readers and watchers sat on the rolling greensward or on curving wooden benches; and beyond, the long municipal pier was crowded with a smooth ebb and flow like the surf itself. There were more sunbathers, more strollers on the shining white sand of the beach. Signs told you the surfs were unsafe, that there were riptides and undertows, but there were still a few waders; there would always be a few waders, a few swimmers, a few challengers.

At one of the benches near the beach, Paige sat down next to an old lady wearing a loose-brimmed straw sun hat. She did not look at him and he did not look at her; he sat with his legs crossed, very relaxed, staring out to sea. I stepped off the wide cinder path and sat down on the lawn under one of the pine trees. I was wearing an old suit, the oldest of the three I owned,

21

and it was of a dark enough color so that grass stains would not show. The walk and the sea air had helped my headache a little, and my chest felt less constricted.

Paige kept on sitting motionless on the bench, communing with the vast Pacific. Out on the rock headlands, cormorants and loons rested between fishing excursions, and even at this distance you could hear the atonal but somehow pleasant barking of sea lions. Near the breakwater, sailboats drifted languidly and a pair of fiberglass ski boats raced side by side, raising fans of white spume not quite as graceful as those created by the skiers they towed behind; and beyond, on the Pacific itself, a charter boat coming in sleek and white against the solid-blue backdrop of sea and sky.

Ten minutes went by. I saw Paige raise his left arm and look at a watch on his wrist and lower the arm again. So all right—he seemed to be waiting for somebody; if you're taking in the air or the sights, you don't usually pay much attention to time. Assuming it was a woman—why here in the park? Why not at the Beachwood, where you could get down to basics in a matter of seconds?

I was good at asking myself rhetorical questions, so I stopped it and tried to blank my mind enough to enjoy the surroundings. Paige glanced at his watch again at one-ten, and again at one-fifteen; other than that, he was very patient sitting there. It began to get a little cool in the shade, and I moved over to a wide patch of sunlight. One twenty-five.

The old woman in the sun hat got up and moved away arthritically. Paige paid no attention to her. But he paid plenty of attention to the wedge-shaped, balding man who took her place on the bench a couple of minutes later; he acknowledged a greeting, slid over a little, and the two of them began an earnest conversation without preamble. I could see their lips moving in profile.

22

I got on my feet, and I did not know what to think. The balding guy was forty, maybe, with heavy masculine features and straight, sparse black hair combed away from the elliptical-shaped bald spot extending from forehead to crown, as if he were proud of it; he wore slacks and a white shirt with the sleeves rolled up on his forearms. Nothing in any of that. Well, maybe it was this alleged business deal, and Judith had been overreacting and I had been too quick to convict Paige before he was proven guilty. But then again, what kind of business do you conduct in the park?

I stood there a little uncertainly. I wanted to hear what they were saying over on the bench, but there was no way I could eavesdrop; the bench was situated on a loop in the path, and one of the rectangles of flowers blocked it off for thirty feet to each side and to the rear. The only thing I could do was walk around in front of them on the path, and there was not much percentage in that, since I would not be able to stop anywhere near them without being conspicuous about it.

But I decided to make the walk anyway. If they were talking loudly enough, there was the chance that I could hear some of their conversation. I took off my suit coat and put it over my right shoulder on my thumb and stepped out onto the path. As I approached, sauntering, trying to look like a guy with nature on his mind and nothing else, they were still sitting with their heads close together. I did not look at them as I passed, and they appeared not to notice me. I could hear the mumble of their voices, but that was all; whatever they were discussing, it was strictly for their own ears.

I followed the path some distance away without looking back, and then turned onto the lawn; there was no point in going back the way I had just come. The two of them were still sitting there, still talking. I located an empty bench facing toward them, under a gnarled old oak, and sat down to wait until they decided to break it up. All I could do now was to keep following Paige, and to wait until something definite happened one way or another.

At the end of another ten minutes the balding guy stood up and turned away to the north, the direction from which he had arrived. Paige stayed where he was for a couple of minutes, watching the sea again; then he got to his feet and moved off to the south. I let him get seventy-five yards away, saw that he was paying no attention to his rear flank, and started after him. He took me directly back to the Beachwood.

I waited outside the motel grounds until Paige was inside his cottage. Then I went over to the office, to where they had a soft-drink machine, and bought myself an orange. I drank it there, letting a few minutes go by. Paige did not come out again. Finally I returned to my own cottage, tossed my coat on the bed, and took up my former position in front of the window.

Time passed, and I began to develop the headache once more. Paige appeared once, forty minutes later, to get something out of his car; other than that, nothing stirred in Number 9. The bamboo blinds were drawn across the cottage's front window, but even if they had been up, I could not have seen inside from where I was, and I had not brought a pair of binoculars with me.

Four o'clock. Five. The sun drifted low over the sea, and the sky turned smoky and bloodshot with lines and streaks of pale crimson. A wind came in off the ocean, gathering strength, and tousled the leaves and needles on the trees. It was quiet in the room—too quiet. I began to feel oddly restless. Nerves. Waiting was never any good, and it was worse when you did not know just what you were waiting for. But the waiting I was having to do was nothing compared to the waiting of Judith Paige—and the half-knowledge for her was agony; for me, only a source of irritation.

24

Five-thirty now, and I was almost out of cigarettes. How much longer? The rest of today, and tomorrow, and part of Monday? Maybe Paige's sole purpose in coming to Cypress Bay was his meeting with the balding guy in the park; maybe that's all there was to it. All right—then why did he tell Judith he was staying until late Monday afternoon this trip out? And what the hell is he doing over in that cottage? Sleeping? Drinking? Watching the goddamn television?

The rear entrance, I thought. The beach entrance.

Oh Christ, I thought. Some stakeout you are, some smart cop. You sit over here on your fat ass thinking visitors have to come in the front way, or that Paige has to go out the front way, and you can't see the rear entrance or the beach and he could be gone or he could be having a party over there with half of Cypress Bay, and even though you can't watch both entrances at the same time, you should have thought about the beach, you should have been checking it . . .

I got up on my feet and went over to the door and cracked it like a furtive neighbor. There was a white-gravel path further down, beyond the office, that led between two of the cottages and onto the private beach. Okay, so let's go out to the beach for a stroll, I thought—and a little voyeurism if you can find a window or a keyhole or a place to put your ear. Play it according to stereotype: the peeper, the snooper. It's that kind of job, isn't it?

I opened the door wide and went out, and the wind was chill on my bare arms; my coat was still inside on the bed. The hell with that too. I started across the grounds toward the gravel path—and all at once the door to Number 9 jerked open, with a sound that was audible above the wind. I managed to keep from breaking stride, but I was looking over there now. The door was still open and it stayed open; Paige did not come out.

I kept on walking, more slowly, and then I stopped because I was almost abreast of the entrance to Number 9 and I could see that there was something in the doorway, something on the floor of the cottage just inside. The wind turned colder. The wind turned very cold.

I had to go over there, and I did it without hesitation. This was something else altogether. I got to the open doorway, and my stomach turned, and the mental image of Judith Paige's sweet pleading face made the sickness in my belly darker and more acute. The waiting was over for all of us now, but for her the agony had only just begun.

If Walter Paige had been an unfaithful husband, he would never be unfaithful again.

And whether or not Judith Paige had been a cuckolded wife, she was now something else entirely: she was a widow.

Four

There was a lot of blood—on Paige, on the floor beneath his body, in a glistening, smeared trail extending half the length of the room. He lay on his back, with one arm outflung toward the door and the other clutched at his upper chest like a bright-red claw. He wore a pair of slacks, nothing more, and his bare, thickly haired chest was soaked and matted with too much blood to make the nature of his wounds easily apparent; but it appeared obvious that he had been stabbed, and more than once.

My stomach kept on turning, but I went inside anyway, avoiding the blood, and got the door closed. The drapes were drawn almost closed across the glass at the rear of the room, and it was dark enough in there to warrant the light burning on the nearer of the two nightstands. I crossed to the drapes and drew them aside and opened the glass door carefully with a handkerchief over my hand.

Outside, there was a kind of patio, enclosed by low cypress hedges; a wood gate opened on a boardwalk leading to the motel's private beach, and the first twenty feet or so of the walk was walled by more of the cypress. I walked out there and tried the latch on the gate; it was unlocked. Beyond, the beach was deserted in both directions, and it had a lonely, hushed look, the way beaches do at sunset; the sand was a reddish-gray in the cold light of the falling sun. The sea seemed restless now, the color of ashes, and there were whitecaps out near the break-water and white froth on the mouths of the combers as they bit into the sand. The wind was like ice on my face.

I went back inside and closed the sliding door again and looked the room over, the way you do automatically if you've been a cop for enough years. There was a thick puddle of con-gealing blood over by the desk, and it looked as if Paige had been stabbed there. He had too much blood in his throat to cry out loudly enough for anyone to hear, I thought, and so he dragged himself across the floor, and got the door open, and died. There was no sign of a weapon, and no indications that a struggle of any kind had taken place; Paige had been killed by someone he knew, or possibly someone who had caught him completely by surprise.

The bed was rumpled, top sheets tossed down at the foot, one of the blankets on the floor; it could have meant something, or it could have meant he had been taking a fitful nap. There was a half-empty pint of Jack Daniel's sour mash and a glass with an inch of dark-amber liquid on the same nightstand with the lamp; the other nightstand held a clean ashtray and the telephone. One of the room's chairs contained Paige's sports jacket and turtle-neck sweater; his socks and shoes were on the floor in front of it. Against the wall next to the desk was a luggage rack with the overnight bag open on top. I stepped to the case and looked in-side without touching anything. There was not much to see: a change of underwear and socks, a second and sealed pint of Daniel's, a clean shirt in a laundry wrapping, and a paperback mystery novel.

The paperback held my attention momentarily. It was torn and dog-eared, with a gaudy cover depicting a half-nude redhead and a guy with a .45 automatic; the redhead's hair-do, and the guy's clothes, and the cover price of twenty-five cents made it obvious that the book was a product of the early fifties. The title was *The Dead and the Dying*, and the author was Russell Dancer. I had never heard of the novel, but the writer's name was familiar. Russell Dancer had been a prolific pulp creator of detective and adventure fiction through the forties and very early fifties, until the complete collapse of the pulp market, and his name was prominently featured on at least a hundred covers among the five thousand pulp magazines which comprised my own collection. But it seemed odd that Paige would have a book like that with the newsstands filled with more modern paperbacks—unless he had been an aficionado of Dancer's work or the field in general . . .

I turned away from the bag. The odor of blood was thickly brackish in there, and my head ached malignantly. I went to the door and outside without looking at Paige again, and made certain the door was unlocked before I shut it. Then I crossed to the motel office.

Orchard was sitting behind the counter, reading the Monterey newspaper. He looked up at me, started to smile, and changed it to a frown when he saw my face. He stood up. "Is something the matter, sir?"

"Yeah," I said. "You'd better call the police, Mr. Orchard."

His eyelids worked up and down like intricately veined fans. "The police?"

"There's been a killing in one of your cottages."

"Killing? Killing?"

"In Number nine," I said. "Walter Paige."

All the color drained out of Orchard's cheeks, and his parted, too-red lips were like an open wound against the sudden marmoreal cast of his face. "Are you sure? A killing—*here*? My God!"

"You can go out and have a look yourself, if you want."

"Oh no, no, I . . . believe you. It's just that . . . Mr. Paige, you say?"

"That's right."

"What happened? How did—?"

"Somebody stabbed him."

"Stabbed . . . him . . ." His eyes widened, and he shrank away from me with his hands fluttering in front of him like restless white doves. "You . . . it wasn't . . . ."

"No," I said, "it wasn't. Listen, will you call the police or do you want me to do it?"

"No," Orchard said, "no, it's my responsibility, I'll call them . . ." The doves came together and mated fretfully, and he turned away and got himself through the doorway into his private office. "A killing . . . we've never had . . . the Beachwood is a respectable family motel . . . oh God, oh my God!"

I went around the counter and watched him at a polished mahogany desk, fumbling with the telephone. It took him thirty seconds to dial seven digits, and a full minute to get two sentences' worth of facts reported thickly into the receiver; but he got the story straight enough, remembering my name and using it freely. When he had finished the call, he put the handset down and began mopping at his face with a yard of silk handkerchief.

I said from the doorway, "How long will it take them to get here?"

"Five minutes, or ten, I don't know."

"We'd better go outside and wait for them."

"Yes. Yes, all right."

We went out, and it was almost dusk. Three-quarters of the sun had fallen beyond the gray rim of the sea; what little light remained had a blood-red tinge. Orchard looked up at the darkening sky and went back inside and turned on the night lighting for the motel grounds—carriage-style lamps on high ivy-

covered poles. The white gravel of the drive seemed lumines-
cent under their glare.

When Orchard came out again, he paced back and forth in
front of the office, worrying his hands. Cottage Number 9
seemed to have a magnetic pull on his eyes. I sat on the topmost
of the three steps that led up to the office entrance, and smoked
my last cigarette.

I said to him, "Is this the first time Paige has stayed here? Or
have you seen him before?"

"What? Oh—no, he's been quite a regular weekend guest."

"For how long?"

"The past month or so."

"Do you know what business he had in Cypress Bay?"

"Of course not. How would I know?"

"I thought he might have mentioned something to you."

"No, he didn't. No."

"Did he have any visitors that you know about?"

"I really don't recall."

"Did you ever see him with a woman?"

"Here? At the Beachwood?"

"Or anywhere else."

"A respectable family motel . . . no, no, certainly not."

"How about a bald guy, forty or so, heavy-featured?"

"No."

"Do you know of any local acquaintances he might have
had?"

"I do not," Orchard said. "See here, why are you asking all
these questions? Did you know Mr. Paige?"

Before I could give him any kind of answer, two black-and-
white police cruisers turned off Ocean Boulevard to enter the
motel grounds; they used no sirens. A third cruiser remained at
the entrance to screen admittance. The first two pulled up to
where Orchard and I were standing, and a couple of uniformed

cops got out of one and two guys in business suits got out of the other.

One of the latter—wearing a dark-brown gabardine—was six and a half feet tall, with iron-gray hair and a long, sad, intelligent face; he was maybe fifty-five, and he walked with long, shambling strides, as if he had never quite learned the art of bodily coordination. His eyes were dark and deep-set, the lids canted sharply, so that when he blinked he had a vaguely Oriental appearance. His name was Ned Quartermain, and he was the Chief of Police of Cypress Bay. The other plainclothes man was a Lieutenant Favor; thin of body, he had unruly brown hair and a thick, incongruous mustache; he reminded me of a silent-movie comedian. But his eyes, like Quartermain's, were shrewd, and you knew immediately there was nothing of the Chaplinesque buffoon about him. He was outfitted with a police camera, a fingerprint kit, and another small technician's kit: a walking crime lab.

Orchard fluttered a little, like a frightened gull, and Quartermain told him to relax; then he said to me, "You're the one who discovered the body?" His voice was soft and faintly sepulchral, but in a way that was not displeasing.

I answered, "Yes."

"Can I see some identification?"

I got my wallet and gave it to him and watched him open it up and find the photostat of my investigator's license. He read it very carefully, and then looked up at me again. "Private detective," he said with no inflection.

"Yes."

"Here on a case?"

"Yes."

"This Walter Paige a part of it?"

"He was all of it."

"You want to give me the details?"

I nodded. "Now—or after you've looked at the body?"

"After. I'll call you down when I want you."

"Whatever you say."

"Number nine, is that right?"

"Yes."

"Door unlocked?"

"Yes."

He made a thoughtful motion with his head and turned and went down there with Favor and one of the uniformed cops at his heels; the other cop, a very young one, stayed with Orchard and me. I watched Quartermain open the door to Paige's cottage, pause, enter with Favor, and shut the door again. A couple of other guests had seen the arrival of the police cars, and were out of their cottages and walking around the way they do, rubbernecking. The second uniform went over to keep them out of the way and available for future questioning.

Some time passed, and none of us said anything. Orchard was pacing up and down again, working on his face with the handkerchief, muttering softly to himself. I tried to keep my mind inactive, but thoughts of Judith Paige kept intruding on the blankness. It would be very bad for her for a while, because death is something you can never cope with as easily as simple infidelity. Guilty of sexual promiscuity, or not guilty of it, Walter Paige was beyond her love or forgiveness or scorn; he was gone, dead, murdered, torn from her violently and without choice. The scars would be deeper now, perhaps more permanent, and some of the fine fresh innocence would be forever lost; she was the little country girl raped by the big city and the California promise —an old story, an old cliché, and it made you feel sour and empty to know that the old stories and the old clichés came about because they were realities of life that happened again and again . . .

An ambulance, without siren and without its red light in operation, pulled onto the motel grounds; behind it was a gray Buick with a single occupant. The young cop went over to tell

them where to go, and they went there; the guy from the Buick
—probably the county coroner or an assistant, judging from the
black bag he carried—rapped on the cottage door and was admitted. The ambulance attendants, in white, stood around out
front and smoked, waiting.

A large crowd had gathered out on Ocean Boulevard, and
the patrol unit had its hands full keeping traffic moving and the
milling people out of the way. The second uniform was still holding the small knot of motel guests off to one side of Number 9.
After a while Quartermain put his head out of the cottage door
and called to the ambulance attendants. They went in with a
stretcher and came out a couple of minutes later with Paige
strapped to it and put him inside the ambulance and took him
away into the night.

Quartermain appeared again and motioned up to me. When
I got down there, he said quietly, "Okay, you can tell your story
now."

So I told him why Judith Paige had hired me, and gave him
her San Francisco address; I explained what I had seen and done
on this day, describing the balding man Paige had met in the
park and relating what Orchard had told me. When I was
finished with all of that, I asked him to be gentle with Judith
Paige when he talked to her; and I told him why.

He studied me for a time. "She must have made quite an impression on you."

"Yeah," I said.

"Well," he said, "you can rest your mind—all right?"

"All right."

"Now let's go over things a little. You didn't see anybody
come or go while you were watching the cottage here, is that
right?"

"Yes."

"And you were at the window the whole time."

"Yes. I didn't even think about the rear entrance until just before I found him. Maybe, if I had, I could have prevented what happened."

"You blaming yourself?"

"There wouldn't be any point in that."

"No, there wouldn't," Quartermain said. "Did you go inside the cottage when you found Paige?"

I nodded. "I thought maybe the killer was somewhere nearby. I went out to the rear, but the beach was deserted."

"Touch anything?"

"No. I used my handkerchief when I went through the sliding door."

"Did you look around inside?"

"A little."

"Notice anything that might help us?"

"I don't think so."

"Okay. Any idea who this bald guy might be?"

"None at all."

"You heard nothing of his conversation with Paige?"

"They had their heads too close together."

"Like old friends?"

"Like that."

"Maybe Mrs. Paige knows him."

"It's possible."

"Did you notice where the guy went when they broke it up?"

"North through the park. I didn't see him leave it. I was concentrating on Paige, and he left a minute or two later."

Quartermain ran a hand through his iron-gray hair and looked at the palm as if he expected to find something there. "I guess that's about all," he said. "Thanks for the cooperation. We appreciate it."

"I was a cop once," I said. "I know how tough it can be."

"San Francisco force?"

"For fifteen years."

"How come you quit?"

"It's a long story," I said. "Look, I imagine you'll want to check me out up there. You can talk to Lieutenant Eberhardt, in General Works. I think he'll vouch for me."

"I'll do that," Quartermain said. "You won't mind remaining here in Cypress Bay for a day or so, will you? Until we clear this thing up a little."

"No, I guess not."

"Drop around to City Hall sometime tomorrow. I'll be there, I think. We'll talk some more—I'll have a statement typed up for you to sign."

"Okay."

He asked me to send Orchard down there, and I said I would; then we nodded to each other, because it was not the kind of situation that called for handshaking, and I returned to the motel office. I relayed Quartermain's request to Orchard, and watched him flutter some more, and then walk down to where the Chief was waiting.

The police guard on the motel entrance allowed a couple of cars to pass through, and as they approached I could see the *Press* cards in their windshields. I did not want to talk to reporters, but there was no way out of the area just yet. I stood there and took it, shielding my face from the cameras and ignoring most of the questions. They got tired of me very quickly, and half of them went down to try to get at Quartermain, and the other half went to the assemblage of motel guests.

I decided I wanted out of there and left the grounds as unobtrusively as I could manage it. I walked along Ocean Boulevard until I came to a small seafood restaurant, ate a bowl of chowder and drank a bottle of beer because I had not had anything to eat since breakfast, and then lingered over a second beer that I did not really want either.

When I finally returned to the Beachwood, things had settled down to normal; the cops and the reporters and the morbid public were gone, and the grounds were hushed and empty. I entered my cottage and lay down on the bed and tried to forget the way Paige had looked lying there with all the blood on him. I could forget that easily enough, I discovered, but the image and the ordeal of Judith Paige was something else again—and it was too many hours before sleep came around to pull down the veil . . .

Five

The phone rang at seven-fifty the next morning.

I had slept maybe four hours, and I was up and shaving in the bathroom. My eyes, in the medicine-cabinet mirror, were shot through with webs of pink and red lines; my lungs were thick with bitter phlegm, and every now and then a spasm of coughing would bring some of it up. I felt gray and irritable, the way you do with a bad hangover. Outside in the garden, sparrows chattered senselessly—and in the distance there was the sound of church bells, like gently imploring words drifting on the sweet spring air. Sunday morning. The loneliest time of the week, if you're alone to begin with. And the Sunday morning following a bad Saturday, a Saturday filled with blood and death and sorrow, is the worst kind of lonely there is.

When the telephone bell went off, I jumped a little and cut myself. I had a fine set of nerves. I tore off a piece of toilet paper and dabbed at the pustule of blood as I went out and hooked the receiver off the unit on the nightstand. I gave my name, and a woman's voice—sweet and low, like the old blues song, and painfully melancholy, too, like the voice of Billie Holiday—said hesitatingly, "I . . . this is Judith Paige."

I tried to think of something to say, but I had no words.

There *are* no words. It was an awkward moment, and I wished she had not called; and yet, I was relieved that she had.

I said finally, to break the deepening stillness, "Are you here in Cypress Bay, Mrs. Paige?"

"Yes. I flew down to Monterey last night, with the San Francisco officer who . . . came to tell me what happened."

"I couldn't call you," I said. "It was out of my hands."

"You mustn't apologize. I understand."

"Did they treat you all right?"

"Everyone has been very kind."

"You talked with Chief Quartermain?"

"Yes. He met us at the airport last night."

"Is there anything . . . definite yet?"

"I don't think so. He promised to tell me as soon as there was." Tremulous breath. "Can I . . . talk to you? I mean, would you come here for a little while?"

I did not want to stand face to face with her grief, but there was no way I could turn her down. "Yes," I said. "Where are you?"

"The Bay Head Inn. Room five."

"I'll be there as soon as I can."

I left the cottage ten minutes later, fully shaved, wearing the same suit but a fresh shirt and underwear. The sunlight was warm and effulgent, and the glare stabbed at my eyes like sharpened fingernails. The day was sharply voluble with the barking of sea lions and the screaming of gulls and cormorants and loons and the drifting sound of distant laughter. The bay was speckled with the whiteness of sails and with golden threads woven by the rising sun. Idyllic Sunday morning: illusion, concealing human folly and human despair. Or maybe I just had a hard-on for the world today.

I crossed to the motel office, and there were two cars just leaving the grounds—travelers moving on, as travelers do, or nervous vacationers fleeing the onus of prolonged association with violent death. I went inside, and Orchard was not on duty; his place had been taken by a plump, matronly woman wearing a bright dress and a brighter smile. If she knew what had happened at the Beachwood the previous night and the part I had played in it—and she must have known—she was not letting on about it. Her greeting was cordial and professional. I told her I would probably be staying another full day, if not the night itself, and got a street map of the area from her and asked her where I could find the Bay Head Inn. She told me, and I found the street on the map; it was a couple of blocks off Grove Avenue, in the heart of the village.

I was there in five minutes, and the inn was an Old Spanish-style building three stories high, with wrought-iron balconies and a tile roof and a whitewashed adobe façade grown with ivy and shaded by tall Monterey pines. A slender clerk told me where Room 5 was located, and I went up a curving iron-railed staircase to the second floor and stopped in front of the door with *Five* spelled out in black iron. I knocked softly. She said my name in there, questioningly; when I confirmed it, she told me to come in, the door was unlocked.

I depressed the antique latch and stepped into a long, large room darkened against the brilliancy of the morning; sunlight and spring, like laughter by the side of a grave, make a mockery of grief. Judith was sitting in a saddle chair studded with black rail-spike heads, her legs tucked under her, her face a white oval in the room's half-light. She wore a simple black dress, and no make-up that I could see; the blond hair was limp, uncombed. She looked like a sad, lost little girl, sitting there that way, her hands folded in her lap. You could sense the feeling of privation in the dark silence, like the essence of vanished youth and faded memories that lingers in the room of a very old gentlewoman.

I shut the door, and she said "Thank you for coming" in that low, painful voice. She watched me as I crossed to the second of

40

the two chairs and sat down and tried to find something to do with my hands.

I said inadequately, "I'm sorry, Mrs. Paige."

"Yes," she said. "I know that."

"Is there anything I can do?"

"That was what I wanted to ask you. Can you . . . help the police in some way?"

I had been afraid of that sort of response to my question, because there was only one answer I could give her. I said, "I don't think so, Mrs. Paige. The authorities don't like private individuals involving themselves in murder investigations. And I have no facilities of my own, even if I could get permission to look into it."

"I see." She looked beyond me, to something only she could see. "Why would anyone kill him?"

"I don't know, Mrs. Paige."

"He had no enemies. He was very easygoing."

You only knew him for a few months, I thought. I said, "The police will find out who it was. And why it was. It will only be a matter of time." The words seemed hollow as I spoke them.

"There's a chance it was a woman, isn't there?"

I couldn't lie to her. "Yes, there's a chance."

"If I knew at least that much," she said, "I might be able to feel something. I don't feel anything now. I mean, I feel numb now. I can't cry any more and I can't think any more."

I said nothing; what can you say?

Seconds went by, like furtive footsteps, and then she said, "I have to know. I don't think I can live with it if I don't know why he died."

"You have to live with it," I said, "with or without the answer. You can't hide from it and you can't run away from it."

"I know. I . . . know."

"What will you do, later on? Will you go back to Idaho?"

"I suppose I will. I have nowhere else to go."

"Do you have family there?"

"Yes."

"They'll make it easier for you, if you let them."

"Thank you, I know they will."

I felt uneasy. "I didn't mean to preach, Mrs. Paige."

"No, you're being very practical. I need that just now."

I wanted my first cigarette of the day, but tobacco smoke would have been as inappropriate in there as the sunlight. I said, "Did the police ask you about the man I saw with your husband yesterday?"

"Several times."

"You don't know him, then?"

"No. I'm very certain I don't."

"And you've never seen a man of that description?"

"Not that I can recall."

"Did your husband mention Cypress Bay at any time?"

She moved her head slightly in a negative way. "I had no idea there was such a place. I had to ask the officer who came last night where it was."

"Did he keep an address book—your husband?"

"No. Walter was . . . well, nongregarious. We didn't have very many friends, you see."

"Was there anything in his effects?"

"Chief Quartermain didn't tell me if there was."

I could not think of anything else of pertinence to say, and she would not want small talk of any kind. I put my hands on the arms of the chair—and I remembered then, for no particular reason or because it had been in the back of my mind all along, looking for a rational escape, about the paperback mystery novel I had seen in Walter Paige's overnight bag. I put voice to the recollection, and then I said, "Did the police ask you about the book, Mrs. Paige?"

"No, they didn't say anything about it. What kind of book is it?"

"A mystery novel—a thing called *The Dead and the Dying* by Russell Dancer."

"The dead and the dying," she said. "That's very appropriate, isn't it?"

"No," I said. I did not want her feeling sorry for herself. "Have you ever seen the book?"

She sighed. "I don't think so."

"Did your husband read much mystery fiction?"

"He didn't read any, that I know of."

"Was he a collector or accumulator of books?"

"No. He didn't seem interested in them at all."

"That makes an odd point, then."

"Do you think it might be important?"

"I don't know. Probably not."

"I don't see how it *could* be."

"Neither do I," I said. "Still, the book is fifteen or twenty years old—and it isn't common for someone to have a paperback of that vintage unless he collects them or reads enough to frequent secondhand stores."

"Should you tell the police about that?"

"I think it would be a good idea," I said. "I have to see Chief Quartermain today and I'll tell him then."

She nodded quietly.

"Were you told when you could leave Cypress Bay?" I asked.

"Not exactly. Chief Quartermain asked me to stay until he makes a more thorough investigation. They're paying for this room, he said. It's a nice room, don't you think?"

"Yes. Look, Mrs. Paige, I'll be here for a while too. I could drive you back to San Francisco if you like, when the time comes."

"Yes, I'd appreciate that. Thank you. You've been very nice about everything. I only wish . . . well, I wish you hadn't had to get involved in a thing like this."

There was no irony in her words, but I could feel an irony just the same—hot and sharp and virulent. I got up on my feet. "I'd better be going now," I said. "Will you be okay here?"

"Yes. You mustn't worry about me."

Somebody was going to have to worry about her—for a while anyway, until she got home to her family in Idaho. I said, "If you want company later on, call me at the Beachwood. Will you do that?"

She inclined her head, and I stood there looking at her a moment longer; but there were no more words for either of us. I turned and went to the door and got out of there—out of dark reality and into the bright world of make-believe.

Six

Cypress Bay's City Hall was one of the Monterey adobe buildings, freshly whitewashed and quietly official behind a lime-green lawn and the inevitable woodsy shade of pines and black oaks. There was a parking lot off to one side, and I took my car in there and left it and went over to the front of the building. To the right of the brick stairs was a small white picket sign, like the ones you see in national parks; it said *Police* on it and had an arrow pointing to a wide brick-paved, pine-needled path. The path led me around to a redwood-roofed wing, fronted by a kind of plaza decorated with wooden planters full of ferns. A much larger sign on the whitewashed facing wall read: *Cypress Bay Police Department.*

I passed through double glass doors and up to a long counter behind which were a modern PBX, a couple of blue-metal filing cabinets, two blue-metal desks, and a fat sergeant with grave brown eyes and jughandle ears. He told me Quartermain was in, checked with him, got an okay for me to see him, and buzzed me through a set of electronically controlled doors on the left. I went down a long corridor, past private offices and interrogation cubicles and file rooms, until I came to a perpendicular hallway that looked as if it ran part of the length of the main

City Hall building. At the apex of the T, there was a door with dark blue lettering that said: *Office of the Chief of Police.*

I entered through there, and a uniformed secretary was banging away on a portable typewriter. In the far wall was a door that had Quartermain's name on it in small blue letters; the secretary told me to go right in.

Quartermain's office was large and comfortable, though more functional than decorative. The carpeting was blue, the walls were white and furbished with framed certificates and a couple of good seascapes; the desk was of flame-swirled walnut, with a glass top, and there were upholstered blue armchairs arranged in front of it and walnut file cases to one side. The only thing that seemed out of place was a very old, dark leather couch against the left-hand wall; but it gave the office a personal touch and told you a little something about Quartermain in the bargain.

He was standing when I knocked and entered. His suit was a loose-fitting oyster-gray today and it made him seem even taller than he was. He thanked me in his soft, sepulchral voice for coming in, and we shook hands this time. I saw then that his eyes were a muted sea-blue, warm or cool depending on the situation—warm now, I thought—and I had the feeling that they were like the shutters on expensive cameras in that they would never miss recording any detail upon which they were focused. Quartermain was every bit the big, shrewd, intelligent cop—but you sensed a gentleness in him, too, an innate fairness; he reminded me a little of Eberhardt, without the falsely sour exterior.

I sat down in one of the armchairs, and Quartermain said, "I've got your statement typed up and ready for your signature." He took a manila folder from one of the four wire baskets on his desk, removed a two-page deposition, and handed it across to me. I read it over and signed it for him and passed it back.

46

I said then, "I was over to see Judith Paige at the Bay Head Inn a little while ago. She phoned me and asked me to stop by."

"I'll be going over to see her myself shortly, more or less unofficially. How is she this morning?"

"Not bad, not good."

"She took the news pretty hard, from what Kanin, the San Francisco inspector who broke it to her, told me last night. He brought her down on the Monterey plane and she seemed to be bearing up; but when she saw her husband in the hospital morgue she went to pieces, and it was a hell of a thing to see. One of the nurses took her over to the inn—she refused to stay at the hospital—and put her to bed with a sedative."

"I suppose this Kanin questioned her about her whereabouts at the time of Paige's death."

"Of course."

"And she checked out clear?"

"Clear enough for me," Quartermain said. "She was baby-sitting three neighbor kids in her apartment; mother and father went to some lodge affair. The kids were old enough to verify her presence in the apartment at the time of the killing."

"There was never any doubt," I said, "as far as I was concerned. She couldn't have killed him. She couldn't kill anyone." I paused. "Have you got a line on the bald man yet—the one I saw with Paige?"

"Not yet. Mrs. Paige says she doesn't know anyone who looks as you described him."

"Yeah, she told me the same thing."

"I'd like you to have a look through our mug files, if you don't mind. I don't suppose there's much chance we'll have a card on the guy, but then again you never know."

"Be glad to," I said, and he led me out and to their Records Room. I spent the next twenty minutes flipping through a not surprisingly small rogues' gallery of men arrested at one time or another in the Cypress Bay area. The bald man was not among them.

Quartermain said, "Well, if we start running into dead ends, I may want you to work with a police artist on a drawing. So far, he's the only definite local link we've got with Paige, and I'd like to know who he is and why the two of them met in the park."

"Fine. Just say the word."

"We'll see how the investigation develops."

We returned to his office and sat down again, and I asked, "Was Paige carrying anything to give you a lead?"

"Nothing. His effects yielded zero."

"Did you find any fingerprints aside from Paige's?"

"Nothing identifiable. There were traces of blood in the bathroom lavatory, which probably means the killer was splashed during the stabbing and took the time to wash some of it off before leaving."

"None of the other motel guests saw anything?"

"If they did, they're not admitting it."

"What about the murder weapon?"

"No sign of it."

"What was it, could they tell?"

"Something long and sharp and fairly thin. Stiletto maybe, or a letter opener of some kind. Along those lines."

"Doesn't sound like you've got much to go on," I said carefully.

"We've got a couple of things." He put his elbows on the desk glass and folded his left fist into his right palm. "I don't suppose I ought to tell you about them, but I gave your Lieutenant Eberhardt a call last night; he was working the four-to-midnight, so I caught him at the Hall of Justice. He has kind words for you, all right."

"Yeah, well, we've been friends for a long time."

"He says you'll cooperate one hundred percent, and you've done that so far. We've got two things to work with on Paige's

48

killing—neither of which have to mean anything, strictly speaking—and maybe you can give me a fresh slant."

"If I can. I appreciate the confidence."

"First of all, we ran Paige's name through R & I in Sacramento as a matter of routine, and came up with a positive. He spent four years in San Quentin out of a seven-year sentence, the usual time off for a clean prison record. He was released about five months ago."

I felt my mouth pull tight. "What was the charge?"

"Burglary. He was convicted in Santa Barbara."

"Does Mrs. Paige know about this?"

"No. At least, I don't think so."

"You're not releasing it to the papers?"

"Hell no," Quartermain said. "But there's always the chance they'll pick it up anyway."

I moved uncomfortably in the chair. "Was Paige lone-wolf on this burglary, or did he have accomplices?"

"Lone-wolf. He tried to pop one of those old-fashioned box safes you still find in some of the older companies—a marine equipment outfit, in this case—and a private security patrol picked him up coming out of the building."

"First offense?"

"Two drunk-driving priors, one in San Francisco and one in the Santa Barbara area. Nothing else in California and nothing in his native Pennsylvania. We're still checking his background."

"What's this other thing you've got?"

"This one isn't very pretty either," Quartermain said. His long face seemed even sadder, and when those canted eyelids came down he resembled a kind of elongated Buddha; some other time it might have been comical. Some other time. "There were semen and vaginal secretions on the bed sheets in Paige's cottage. He was with a woman not long before he was killed."

It did not surprise me; I had been waiting for it all along. I lit a cigarette and coughed and stared through the smoke, and I could see her sitting in that saddle chair, curled up in the darkness, grieving—for an ex-convict, a son-of-a-bitching womanizer. Why? Because love is blind, and he was handsome and probably glib, and she was just that little country girl looking for happiness and security and affection. And Paige? Well, you could figure his motivations simply enough as far as their marriage was concerned: if you can't score one way, and you want to score badly enough, you can always come up with a proposal and a ring; then, when you're tired of the innocence and the responsibility—tired enough to want out of the union—you go to the accommodating California divorce courts and dissolve the whole thing with a minimum of difficulty . . .

I said, "So she came in from the beach while I was watching the front, and they were banging away in there the whole time." The words sounded harsh and bitter.

"It figures that way," Quartermain agreed. He rubbed wearily at his temples. "The thing that we can't know yet is whether she left and then Paige was killed by someone else, or whether she killed him herself."

"If it was somebody else, that rear entrance was a regular goddamned concourse."

"The woman might not have wanted to be seen. Coming in that way would lower the risk. Paige must have called her from the phone in his cottage to let her know which one he was in."

"No clues at all to her, I guess?"

"None. Ashtrays were all clean, and there were no tissues or any other feminine items. If it hadn't been for the bed, we'd never even know she was there."

"I remember seeing half a bottle of Jack Daniel's and a glass on one of the nightstands," I said. "How about another glass?"

"None in the cottage."

"So she didn't drink. Or they shared the same glass, and she

50

had her lipstick scrubbed off. Or she took the damned thing with her when she left."

"Or the killer took it, if it wasn't the woman."

Neither of us cared for further speculation, and more silence built between us. I put fire to another cigarette; the first one was still smoldering in the abalone-shell tray on Quartermain's desk. At length I said, "I don't know if this means anything, but I thought I'd better mention it to you. Did you notice the paperback book in Paige's bag?"

"I noticed it. Why?"

I related my conversation with Judith Paige, and Quartermain looked thoughtful for a time. He said finally, "Well, I admit that it might be pretty odd for Paige to have a book that old if he wasn't a reader or a collector, but I don't see what it could have to do with his death. And there's another thing, too: the book might not have been his."

"It was in his bag."

"Sure, but we had that woman in the cottage. She might have left it."

"From what was found on the sheets," I said, "the two of them weren't doing any damned reading."

"It could have been in her purse, and she could have put the purse on his bag, and it could have fallen out accidentally. That's just one possible explanation."

I thought it over. "It could have happened like that, I guess."

"I examined the book myself," Quartermain said, "after Lieutenant Favor got through taking print smudges off the covers. It's just a book, pretty well beat up but with all the pages intact and no markings on it—nothing underlined or written on the margins, like that. Just a book."

"So you're not holding it as evidence?"

"I don't see any point in it. I'll release it with Paige's effects later today."

"How long will you want Mrs. Paige and me to remain in Cypress Bay?"

"Today at least, in case anything comes up. You can both leave tonight if nothing does—and if we need that drawing of the bald guy, you can work with one of the artists on the San Francisco force."

I nodded. "Can I ask a small favor, then?"

"I guess that would depend on the favor."

"I'd like to have the book."

"Now?"

"Yes."

"Why?"

"I don't really know," I said. "Maybe because I happen to collect pulp magazines, and this Russell Dancer is an old pulp writer—or maybe because I can't quite put it out of my mind."

"Pulp magazines," Quartermain said. "I used to read those when I was a kid."

"So did I. But I never got over them. In a way, they were the reason I became a cop."

"Well, I guess everybody has to have a hobby." He smiled faintly. "I don't see any reason why you can't have the book. Mrs. Paige isn't going to want it."

"No," I said.

"But you'll keep it available, just in case?"

I said I would, and Quartermain inclined his head and got up on his feet. He was some big guy, all right. He came around his desk, said, "I'll have to go down to the property room," banged my shoulder in a friendly way, and shambled out.

I sat there in the silence, smoking and waiting and trying to control the irrational rage I was building up toward a dead man I had scarcely known at all. So he was a son of a bitch, so he was an ex-con, the world is full of both kinds and both combinations, you can't change the goddamn world. But even though I kept telling myself that, cynically, it was plain fact that Judith Paige had stirred my paternal embers, and I could not get her and this whole affair out of my system. It would take a while, and then there would be ghosts—the way there were ghosts of Erika and Cheryl and some others too . . .

Quartermain came back with the copy of *The Dead and the Dying*, and I glanced at it briefly and put it into the pocket of my suit coat. He said, "I'll give you a call at the motel when it's all right for you and Mrs. Paige to return to San Francisco, or if I need you again. In either case, you should hear from me late this afternoon sometime."

"Okay," I said. "Thanks, Chief."

We clasped hands again and I went over to the door. I had just gotten it open when Quartermain said, "What do you think she'll do now? After this thing is finished, I mean?"

"I don't know," I said. "Maybe she'll go back to Idaho."

"That would be the best thing for her."

"I think so, too. San Francisco is a nice city but it's no place for little girls from Idaho."

"Look, why don't you keep an eye on her for a while—until she goes home? She could use a friend."

"I was planning on it." I looked at him soberly. "You sound as if she made an impression on you, too."

"Yeah," he said in a grave voice. "Yeah, I guess she did."

When I got back to my cottage at the Beachwood, I looked at the four walls briefly and then went out into the private rear garden and sat on one of the wooden picnic chairs they had there, in the shade of a cone-heavy Bishop pine. I took the copy of *The Dead and the Dying* out of my coat pocket and turned it over and read the back-cover blurb. It went this way:

A Little Peace and Quiet . . .

Johnny Sunderland came home to California from the

bloody battlefields of Korea with a game leg and a bellyful of war. All he wanted was a little peace and quiet. What he got was a fast trip to a hell that made Korea look like a Sunday School picnic!

First he met Nora, who drank too much and played too hard—and died too easy. Then there were Bernie and Alf, a couple of little men with big .45s. Next came Therm, who would do anything for the likes of two hundred grand—including the murder of his wife. Then Ritter, the sadistic cop who had more on his mind than his job; Hallinan, the horseplayer who lost his one big bet, his nerve, and his life all in one day; and finally, there was Dina, the flaming redhead whose arms promised unlimited passion—or sudden death!

Before he had been home two days, Johnny Sunderland was plunged into a nightmare of murder, treachery, and big-time crime. The object of a massive manhunt conducted by the police on one side and several desperate men on the other, Johnny ran and ran hard. But it wasn't long before he found out that the road he thought would take him to freedom was nothing more than a dead end; and that he was running on a treadmill to oblivion . . .

Pretty lurid stuff; I wondered about the book itself. I opened it up and looked at the inside blurb, which is usually a short cut of narrative from the novel. The heading there read: DRESSED FIT TO KILL, and the first line was: *She came into his room wearing nothing but the smell of her perfume and a .45 automatic.* Well. I turned the page, saw that the copyright date was 1954, and turned another page to Chapter One.

I read the first five pages and put the book down. None of the fast, wacky flair which had characterized Russell Dancer's pulp stuff in *Dime Detective, Detective Tales, Black Mask, Argosy,* and the others; he had had this series character, a private eye named Rex Hannigan, and I had found a lot of redeeming features and a kind of cockeyed charm in Hannigan. Johnny Sunderland was pretty much of a wise-cracking ass, war hero and game leg notwithstanding. But there was one thing about the book, and that was its setting; the cover blurb had mentioned only California, but San Francisco was the stated locale.

I remembered then that all of the early Hannigan stories had been set in New York City, but that around 1950 Dancer had moved him out to San Francisco and environs. I thought about that, and I wondered if the reason for the move was because Dancer himself had come west. Then I began to wonder if Dancer had lived in San Francisco, since he had set the later pulp stories and this novel there; and then I began to wonder where Dancer was *now*, if he was still around and still writing, and if so, where he was.

An idea got itself into my head and kept working away in there. Suppose Russell Dancer—assuming the name was not pseudonymous—lived not in San Francisco but in Cypress Bay or somewhere else on the Monterey Peninsula? Suppose Paige had had the book because, somehow, he knew Dancer? It was a long shot in several different ways, and even if it were possible, it did not have to mean anything in terms of Paige's murder; but it was a nagging little idea, the kind that keeps after you until you do something about it one way or another.

So I got up and went inside and found a telephone directory for the Monterey Peninsula, in the bottom of the nightstand which contained the phone. I opened it up to the D section and ran my finger down the page, and there was a listing for an R. Dancer, on Beach Road, County. That put the idea to work a little harder inside my head. I picked up the phone and dialed the listed number, and after three rings a recorded voice came on and told me the number had been disconnected.

I frowned and closed the directory and looked at the copy of *The Dead and the Dying*. Then I got up and walked around the room for a while. R. Dancer, I thought, Beach Road, County. Well, all right—you haven't got anything else to do today, and if you sit around here you'll do nothing but think about Judith Paige up in that dark room, grieving, and there's nothing in that, you know there's nothing in that. But there may be something in this R. Dancer, if he *is* the writer; and if he is, and there isn't any connection with Paige, you can still talk pulps with him; you've always wanted to meet a pulp writer, haven't you? Go on, get out of here.

I got out of there.

Seven

The coastline south of Cypress Bay was scalloped with jagged cliffs and jutting promontories and deep canyons—the most beautiful coastline in the state, and perhaps on the entire Pacific shore. Monterey cypress trees, native only to this area, their branches and dark-green foliage shaped by the sea winds into grotesquely appealing forms, stood like old, old watchmen atop the bare erosions of rock. The blue-green sea, calm and sun-streaked to the horizon, found a restless energy approaching land and flung itself against the cliffs in a churning froth of foam and spray, as if it harbored a kind of deep-seated resentment for the impassive solidarity of its boundaries. Fat brown pelicans and oyster catchers and pigeon guillemots dotted the headlands and rock islands, and there were glimpses of low-tide beaches teeming with sponges, anemones, crabs, starfish, sea urchins, and beds of golden kelp. It was everything you could want in the way of scenic splendor—or it would have been if there were no oil slicks and garbage dumps and beer cans and toilet paper and cardboard boxes and condoms and litter bags; if humanity had not spread the diseased wastes of its "civilization" like a plague over the land . . .

Beach Road was a narrow paved lane that turned off Highway 1 six miles below Cypress Bay and dropped on a sharp incline toward the ocean. Three or four bungalows and a small trailer encampment were interspersed among dense stands of pine. Rural mailboxes on wooden poles lined the road, but the largest number was 27 and the phone directory had listed R. Dancer at 31. I drove to the end of the lane—a fifth of a mile from the highway—and found myself on a sort of convex bluff face, half-mooned at the edge by low white guardrails mounted with reflectors. Over on the left was an old Ford wood-sided station wagon, drawn up near the head of a set of wood-railed steps leading down to the sea; the number of the mailbox there was 31.

I parked in the dappled shade of one of the large cypress growing there and walked to the stairs, the clean, pungent smell of salt in my nostrils. Once there, I could see the dwelling built on a long sand-and-rock shelf some fifty feet below; the shelf tapered downward into an irregular-shaped, driftwood-strewn beach bounded on both sides by projections formed of a series of eroded, bird-limed boulders—like natural stone jetties extending into the Pacific. The structure was a kind of shack, heavily weathered, fashioned of redwood shingles and beams that had withstood the elements for a long while, but which would not withstand them a great deal longer. It was raised off the shelf on concrete blocks, with gap-toothed lattice board to cover the open spacing; a tired-looking catwalk was attached to the right wall, leading onto a sort of sun porch across the rear width. There was a short walk in front, log-railed like the catwalk and porch, which led from the bottom of the steps to the shack's door; the property was otherwise unadorned, save for a carpeting of sand and small bits of driftwood that had been blown back against the bluff by the wind.

I went down the wooden steps, hanging onto the handrail and moving carefully. The angle of them was not steep, but there was a thin coating of sand on each, and the boards were old and loose. An exposed network of water piping ran down the side of the bluff alongside the steps, and there were power lines that looped down from overhead. I wondered irrelevantly if Dancer's phone had been disconnected because he could not or would not pay his bill.

When I reached the bottom of the steps and started along the sandy walk, I could hear the steady, rhythmic clacking of typewriter keys from inside the shack. I looked for a doorbell, did not find one, and rapped sharply on the heavy door. The typewriter maintained its rhythm. There was a window beside the door, but jalousied shutters were drawn over it and I could not see inside. I knocked again, loudly this time.

Another ten seconds went by, and I was getting ready to knock a third time; but then the keys fell silent and I could hear steps approaching within. The door opened jerkily, under an irritated hand, and I was looking at a thin guy in his early fifties dressed in an old pullover sweater and blue Levi's and white canvas sneakers. He had a shaggy mane of dust-colored hair, clean-shaven if faintly hollowed cheeks, a wryly crooked mouth, and a long Grecian nose marbled by whiskey veins. His eyes were a liquidy blue-gray under thick dust-colored brows that formed lopsided, inverted V's on his forehead, and they were not particularly friendly at the moment.

He looked me over, decided I was nobody he knew, and said, "Well? What is it?"

"Are you Russell Dancer—the writer?"

"No, I'm Russell Dancer—the hack. There's a hell of a big difference. What do you want?"

"I'd like to talk to you, if you wouldn't mind."

"I would mind. I'm working right now."

"It won't take very long."

"You wouldn't be a goddamn bill collector, would you?"

"No," I said. "I'm a private detective."

He stared at me. "A what?"

"A private detective."

"Are you putting me on?"

I got my wallet out of my coat pocket and opened it to the photostat of my license and let him look at it. He read it over twice, ran a prominently veined hand through his shaggy hair, and said, "Well, I'll be damned. You sure as hell don't look like a private dick."

"What does a private dick look like? Rex Hannigan?"

He gave me the stare again. "You remember Rex Hannigan?"

"Sure. Why not?"

"I haven't written a Hannigan story in twenty years."

"I read one a couple of weeks ago."

"Where?"

"In a copy of *Dime Detective*."

"How did you come across that?"

"I collect pulp magazines."

"A private eye that collects pulp magazines," Dancer said. He shook his head wonderingly, but his eyes were friendlier now. "And the first person I've met in fifteen years who admits to reading the Hannigan stories. Christ, most people won't admit to reading anything I ever wrote; who wants to confess that he wastes his time on hack work?"

"I don't think Hannigan was hack work," I said.

"No? Well, Hannigan was the product of a young snot who thought he had some revolutionary ideas about detective fiction that would shake up the industry. The new Hammett, the new Chandler. Yeah. Then he woke up one morning with the truth in his mouth like the taste of vomit: his ideas were old and imitative, and he was not anywhere near as good as he thought he was. After he got over the shock of that, he sold himself out and he sold out what there was of Hannigan for the almighty dollar. He became a prolific hack and he moved to California—it might

60

have been anywhere in the world—and he lived unhappily thereafter. End of story."

"Well," I said.

"Yeah," he said. His mouth turned wolfish. "So what brings a private eye to an ex-creator of private eyes? Don't tell me my former wife is trying to stir up trouble again? The bitch likes to put the shaft in my behind whenever she can, but this would be going a little far—even for her."

"It's nothing like that."

"You might as well come in and tell me what it is, then. The longer you're here, the longer I'm going to believe you were actually here."

He turned, and I followed him inside and down a short hallway with an open kitchen on one side, and on the other, two closed doors that would lead to a bedroom and a bathroom. The entire rear half of the dwelling was a single room, and its end wall was mostly glass that looked out on the sun porch and the Pacific beyond; on the right, a closed door gave access to the porch. The room itself was chaotic. Unpainted tier-type bookshelves—the kind you put together yourself—covered the right-hand wall, but there were more books and magazines strewn on the floor in front of it and around it than there were on the shelves. Against the other wall was a long, narrow redwood plank mounted on two old-fashioned beer kegs; on the plank was a portable typewriter, a stack of manuscript pages in a wire basket, and a farrago of pens, pencils, sheets of paper, and overflowing ashtrays. The remainder of the room's appointments included an old mohair couch, a wicker armchair with an attached footrest, and a stack of cardboard boxes which seemed to serve as filing cabinets.

Dancer said over his shoulder, "Some place, isn't it? Writers are slobs; not Bohemians, just slobs."

I thought of my own apartment in San Francisco; writers

were not the only ones who were slobs. I said, "It's not so bad."

"My ex-wife couldn't stand it. She didn't like anything about this place. To tell you the truth, I don't like it much myself any more. When I bought it in '52, I thought it was arty as hell; you know, the writer living in a beach shack and all that horseshit. Now the sound of the sea gives me a perpetual headache and disturbs my concentration. I'm getting old, I guess—old and tired."

And bitter, I thought. But I could understand some of the way he felt, some of the reasons why. There was a certain loneliness in him, too—the kind that came as the result of vanished dreams and painful understanding of individual limitations—and loneliness is a corroding substance inside a man. I found myself liking him in a kindred sort of way—and because he seemed honest; in a world filled with phonies, you did not meet many honest men.

He asked, "How about a beer?"

"Thanks. I could use one, I think."

"Bottle all right?"

"Sure."

He went down the hallway again and into the kitchen. I wandered over to the writing table, the way you do, and I was looking at one of the manuscript pages lying face up beside the typewriter when Dancer returned with two bottles of Lucky Lager. He handed me one and said, indicating the rough-typed page, "Dancer's answer to *The Ox-Bow Incident*. I call it *Gunsmoke on the Brazos*, and I do two a year in the same vein for one of the cheaper paperback houses."

"I didn't know you wrote westerns," I said.

"I write anything they'll pay me to write. Crime stuff, westerns, Gothics, confession stories, juvenile sports novels, an occasional soft-core porno when the cupboard gets especially bare. I stay alive because after thirty years in the business, I'm like a machine—I can turn out fiction in any field, with any style and slant. The poor bastards who've really got something to say can't say it because the markets are glutted with stuff by guys like me—guys who haven't had anything worthwhile to say for too goddamn many years. But that's not the really tragic thing; the really tragic thing is that literature, fiction, printed matter itself is dying. It's being phased out by television and computers and space-age thinking; the writer, and especially the professional writer, is a vanishing breed—like the kit fox and the bison. In twenty years or so, we'll be in a class with hansom cabs and surreys and buggy-whip manufacturers. I hope to Christ I never live to see it."

I was not sure I went along with that kind of thinking, but then he was in a position to know more about it than me; it was a depressing theory, anyway. I said as much—and then I said, "If this were some other time, some other day, I'd be damned interested in why you think the way you do on the subject, Mr. Dancer; but right now, I'd better get to the point of my visit." I was thinking about Judith Paige again.

"Sure, I understand," he said, and shrugged.

"It has to do with one of your books."

"Yeah? Which one?"

"*The Dead and the Dying.*"

He drank some of his beer, frowned, and shook his head. "I've written maybe sixty novels, and I can remember the title of about six, offhand. That's not one of them. It sounds like a crime thing, but I haven't done a crime novel in more than five years. How far back does it go?"

"It was published in '54, by Onyx Books."

"I sold Onyx a lot of stuff, as I recall. That was one of the reasons they went broke in the late fifties. *The Dead and the Dying.* Well, why would a book published in '54 bring a private detective to see me?"

"There was a killing in Cypress Bay last night," I said. "Did you hear about that?"

"A killing—you mean a murder?"

"Yes."

"No, I didn't hear about it," Dancer said. "I'm coming on the end of the western, and I haven't been out of here in two days; and when I'm working I don't listen to the radio. What does a book of mine have to do with a murder?"

"It was found in the dead man's overnight bag."

"The hell you say!" Dancer was incredulous. "What's this guy's name?"

"Walter Paige."

"Paige—Walter Paige." He rubbed his free hand over the back of his neck, frowning. "Well, I don't know. I knew a guy named Walt Paige once, about five or six years ago."

I released the breath I had been holding. "Where?"

"Cypress Bay."

"How well did you know him?"

"Not very. He was a kind of drinking companion. We used to make the rounds together, along with a bunch of other regulars at the Mount Royal Bar—a place near Carmel Highlands. That's where I met him, at the Mount Royal. He was a smooth, glib bastard, one of these Errol Flynn types with the women. I didn't like him much."

I described Walter Paige. "Is that the guy you knew?"

"It sounds like him, all right," Dancer said.

So we've got a connection now, I thought; but what else have we got? I said, "Did Paige know you were a writer?"

"Sure. But he didn't seem particularly interested. All he cared about, as far as I could see, was pussy and money."

"Then you don't have any idea why he would have one of your old books?"

"Christ no—not one that was written twelve years or so before I ever knew him."

"What about the others in this group you mentioned?" I asked. "Did you know any of them back in '53 or '54?"

"No. This was a pretty young crowd, aside from me."

I pulled at my beer reflectively. There didn't seem to be anything of import in the copy of *The Dead and the Dying* itself—and yet it had thus far led to a tie-up with the author, Russell Dancer, and a link six years in the past between Walter Paige and Cypress Bay. I said, "How long was Paige in this area originally?"

"Six or seven months, I think."

"What kind of job did he have?"

"None, that I knew of. But he was always flush."

"Like that, huh?"

"Like that," Dancer agreed.

"Where did he live?"

"Cypress Bay somewhere, I think."

"Why did he leave, do you know?"

Dancer shrugged. "They come and they go."

"Any idea where Paige went?"

"Seems to me somebody said he'd headed south."

"To Santa Barbara maybe?"

"Could be. Does Paige tie up there?"

"Uh-huh. He took a fall for burglary and spent four years in San Quentin. He got out five months ago."

Dancer pursed his lips sardonically. "Nice company I used to keep."

"Have you heard anything from him or about him since he left those six years ago?"

"Not a word. I'd forgotten all about him. Hell, why would he come back after all these years?"

"It might have been for a woman. There were indications."

"I can imagine what they were," Dancer said. "You figure this woman did for him?"

"Possibly."

"Well, if so, she probably had plenty of provocation."

"Yeah," I said. "Were there any females in this group you and Paige were part of?"

"Sure. It was pretty free-wheeling."

"Some were more regular than others, though?"

"A kind of nucleus, you mean?"

"More or less."

"Two, I guess."

"Was Paige involved with either of them?"

Dancer shrugged again. "If so, they weren't talking and neither was he. I'll say this for Paige—he didn't brag up his conquests."

"Is the group still active?"

"No, not for a long time. You know how those things go."

"Do the two women still live in Cypress Bay?"

He nodded. "But I don't see either one committing murder."

"Maybe not, but they might be able to offer a lead."

"I suppose so."

"Can you give me their names?"

"Robin Tolliver is one. She married an artichoke heir named Jason Lomax, not long after Paige left. They've got an estate on Cypress Point. Robin was never any dummy."

I wrote the names on the note pad I carry.

Dancer said, "The other girl is Bev Winestock. I saw her a few weeks ago. She's still single and still a looker, and still living with her brother in an old place in the town proper. The brother, Brad, used to join the group once in a while."

"Were there any other regulars—people who might have known Paige fairly well?"

"A guy named Ben Simms, but he was killed in a boating accident about five years ago. And Rose Davis got married and moved east maybe three years back. Keith Tarrant is still around, though. He's Cypress Bay's largest realtor now, and owns a sweet pad over in Carmel Valley. When I knew him, he was still struggling for a toehold. The demand for land in this

66

area, and some smart maneuvering on Tarrant's part, put him where he is today. His wife, Bianca, used to come with him sometimes, too. That's about all, except for occasionals, and I can't remember any of them offhand. I've got a lousy memory, anyway."

I wrote the Winestocks and the Tarrants into my notebook. Dancer said then, "Listen, how do you fit in with Paige and his murder?"

"He married a young girl from Idaho in San Francisco a few months ago," I said. "Then he started leaving her alone on weekends, and she figured he'd found another woman. She hired me to follow him. I tailed him down to Cypress Bay yesterday and camped in a cottage across from his at the Beachwood motel. But this woman he had—and the killer, if it wasn't the woman—came in through the rear entrance. I found the body a little later."

"Pleasant little story."

"Isn't it."

"But it doesn't surprise me much. So you're working with the local cops then?"

"Not exactly."

"Lone-wolfing for the wife?"

"Not that either," I told him. "I just had a hunch about *The Dead and the Dying*, and I decided to follow it through. Chief Quartermain is handling the investigation, and I'll turn what you've told me over to him."

"Sure," Dancer said. "You know, Paige having one of my books is going to bug hell out of me. I can figure most of the story, from what I knew of him, but I can't figure the book. You really think it ties in somehow?"

"I don't know," I said honestly.

"Well, if you find out, give me the word, would you?"

"I'll tell Quartermain to give you the word. I'll be going back to San Francisco with Mrs. Paige—probably tonight."

"She's a nice kid, this Mrs. Paige?"

"Yeah," I said. "She's a nice kid."

"And you're not going to follow through?"

"It's out of my hands and out of my league."

"Well, you live and learn," Dancer said. "This is my day to learn about private dicks."

I finished my beer and thanked him for his help, and we went out to the front walk. We shook hands there, and he said, "If you're ever in this area again, drop in and say hello. We could break a couple of six-packs and talk about the pulps. I knew quite a few pulp editors and writers in New York in the forties."

There was a kind of wistfulness in his voice, a nebulous request, of which Dancer himself might not have been consciously aware. You knew Rex Hannigan, his eyes said to me, you liked him, you remembered—and even though the plots and the characters and the words themselves were mere echoes now, all but forgotten by Russell Dancer and by the world at large, there was somebody who remembered and somebody who cared, and that was somehow very important. Deep down where a man lives, he did not want to lose his newly discovered, and perhaps final, touch with the old dream.

I said, "I'll do that," and I meant the words sincerely.

Eight

I drove back into Cypress Bay, parked in the lot next to the City Hall, and went around to the police-station wing. The fat sergeant told me Quartermain had gone to Salinas, the county seat, and that Lieutenant Favor had gone with him; no, he had no idea when they would be back, did I want to leave a message?

Without thinking about it, I said, "No, I'll stop by later," and walked slowly back to my car. I sat there in the cool shade and brooded a little. Well, I could have given it to the sergeant; but it was somewhat involved and Quartermain was the Chief and handling the case personally, and he was the kind of guy I could tell it to in my own way. There was that—and there was Judith Paige, and the quiet tranquillity of Cypress Bay that became almost oppressive after a while, and the restlessness which seemed to be steadily growing inside me. If you've been a cop in one form or another for most of your life, and if you've worked at it and cared for it and been pretty good at it, it bothers you to have to back out of something when there are things to be done, avenues to be explored. It was a little like being a good, well-trained bird dog; once you had the scent, you were not satisfied until you were plowing along the trail and trying to flush something out of the underbrush.

I lit a cigarette and blew smoke through the open window and watched it float languidly like an ephemeral mist through the sunlight and the shadows. *"It's out of my hands and out of my league,"* I had told Russ Dancer, but that was not quite true and I knew it was not quite true, and I kept on sitting there, restlessly, trying to make up my mind. But it was not really much of a struggle. When you're overstepping just a little, the rationalizations come easy; and since you know you're going to do it, and have known it from the moment you found out Quartermain was in Salinas, it only takes a couple of mental nudges to get you to admit it.

So I started the car and drove two blocks to a stone-and-redwood complex that did not look much like a service station, in keeping with the edicts of the Cypress Bay Chamber of Commerce. I parked under a sloping awning that did not quite conceal the row of gasoline pumps, told the attendant to fill up the tank, and went over to the telephone booth. I looked up the addresses for Jason Lomax, Brad and Beverly Winestock, and Keith Tarrant, and wrote them down on my note pad. Then I came back and paid the attendant and looked over the street map. The closest of the three seemed to be the Winestocks, on a street called Bonificacio Drive that was about ten blocks distant.

I went over there, and the house was a two-story Spanish adobe set back some distance from the street, on higher ground. You got up to it by way of twenty-five or thirty slab-stone steps grown with rock cress; at their top was a short arbor covered by reddish bougainvillaea. It was cool and quiet on the narrow porch formed by a wood-railed gallery at the second-floor level —and I thought for no particular reason of Old Monterey, Old California, and what it must have been like to have lived in the days of the Bear Flag and the sprawling ranchos. Dull and simple, maybe—but the air and the land and the sea were clean then, and there were no great external pressures, and you could take your time about living. I tugged at the hand-woven bell pull

70

located to one side of the front door, and listened to a dull, distant ringing within, like a melancholy elegy for the long-dead past.

Pretty soon the door opened and a woman in her early thirties looked out at me. She had a kind of misty beauty, enhanced by moist dark eyes and a pensive mouth and long brown-black hair parted in the middle and swept over her shoulders and down her back, like a dusky tapestry woven of very fine thread and fringed across the bottom. When you looked at her long enough, you had the feeling that she was somehow two-dimensional—an image that could and would vanish wraithlike whenever she chose. But it could have been the shaded porch and the dark shadows behind her, inside the house, that conveyed the impression, or it could have been my mood. She was heavy-breasted and flare-hipped in dark-green cotton slacks and a lime-green shirt, and I found myself thinking—the way a man does sometimes, with this kind of woman—that she would be pure sweet hell in bed.

I brushed the thought aside and put on a polite smile for her. "Miss Winestock?"

She nodded. I gave her my name, and then I said, "I wonder if I might talk to you for a few minutes? It's rather important."

She looked at me steadily. "You're the man who found Walter Paige last night, aren't you? The private detective?"

Her voice was cool and matter-of-fact, and it gave substance to her and destroyed some of the ephemeral quality. I said, "Yes, that's right."

"I heard about it on the midnight news. Is that why you're here?"

"Yes."

"I expected someone would be, sooner or later," she said. "How did you get my name?"

"From Russ Dancer."

"Mmmm," she said without inflection.

"There was an old paperback book of his among Paige's effects," I told her. "One called *The Dead and the Dying*. The police released it to me earlier today, and I followed up a hunch that led me to Dancer."

"Now what would a man like Walt Paige be doing with one of Russ's books?"

"That's one of the things I'd like to know."

"Doesn't Russ have any idea?"

"No, he doesn't."

"I didn't even know Walt could read," she said, and smiled faintly. "Well, won't you come in?"

"Thank you, Miss Winestock."

"Beverly," she said. "I'm not quite an old maid, and Miss Winestock makes me sound like one."

"Beverly," I said.

She took me inside and down an arched hallway hung with Spanish murals and into a tile-floored parlor, darkly furnished. There, she asked, "Would you like a drink? I think we have some beer and wine in the refrigerator; we're out of anything stronger at the moment, I'm afraid."

"Nothing, thanks."

I sat down on a tapestried-cloth sofa and she took the chair across from me and crossed her ankles and smoothed her hands along her upper thighs in a gesture that was sensual and yet seemingly unaffected. I kept my eyes on her face as she said, "There's not very much I can tell you about Walt Paige. I didn't know that he was back in Cypress Bay, and I wouldn't have cared if I had. And I have no idea who could have killed him, though God knows, enough people might have had justification. He was a thorough bastard, you know."

"So I've learned," I said. "How well did you know him when he lived here originally?"

"Not as well as he would have liked."

"Did you ever talk to him about personal matters?"

The faint smile again. "His or mine?"

"His."

"Not really. Russ told you about our group, didn't he?"

"Yes."

"Well, we were a winy bunch. Laughter and liquor, and never a serious moment. At least, not while the group was together. And that's the only place I ever saw Walt Paige, though he tried to change that enough times."

"Do you have any idea who he might have been involved with?"

"Who he was sleeping with, you mean?"

"Well—yes."

"Half the women in Cypress Bay and vicinity, no doubt. He had no morals, and general tastes."

"Any one woman more than another?"

"If so, I never knew about it."

"How about Robin Lomax—or Tolliver at that time?"

Beverly laughed softly; it was the kind of laugh that put cool fingers on your spine and made you think of warm, dark bedrooms. She said, "I doubt it. Robin was hardly a virgin when she married Jason Lomax, although she'd like everybody to think so; but she was more or less going with Jason when Walt Paige was here, and she paid no more attention to Walt than I did. I think we both saw him for exactly what he was."

"I see."

"Do the police think it was a woman who killed him? Is that why you're asking about his former love life?"

"There's a good possibility of it," I said. "He was seeing a woman here in Cypress Bay recently."

"Are there any clues as to who she is?"

"Not at the moment."

"What makes you think she's someone he knew six years ago? Passions cool considerably in six years—unless, of course, he was seeing her fairly regularly since then."

"He didn't see her for at least four years, except maybe on visitors' day."

"I don't think I understand."

"Walter Paige spent four years for burglary in San Quentin," I said. "He was released five months ago."

She frowned deeply. "I didn't know that."

"Does it surprise you?"

"Not much, I guess. I always wondered where he got the money he used to spread around so freely. Was he arrested around here?"

"No. In Santa Barbara."

"Maybe he just never got caught in this area."

"Maybe not."

She moved restlessly on her chair. "Well, if any woman waited four years or more for Walt Paige, she's the biggest fool in creation. Or just plain blind."

"That happens—too often."

"Don't I know it!" Beverly said. "The radio mentioned that Walt had a wife and that you were doing some kind of job for her. Did it have to do with this woman, the one here in Cypress Bay?"

"Yes. He'd been leaving his wife alone on the weekends, and she wanted to know why."

"And now she knows."

"Not yet. She isn't ready to know."

"She must be taking it pretty hard."

"Pretty hard."

"What's she like?"

"Nice. Very nice and very young."

"I thought she might be. That's the only kind of woman Walt Paige would have bothered marrying. She'll be all right, though; you learn to accept the crap life deals out to you."

"Sometimes you do."

"You have to if you want to get along in this world," Beverly said. "Voice of experience."

"Has it been that rough for you?"

"And then some. I've led a hell of a life." She shrugged. "But then, I've made my own bed most of the time—literally as well as figuratively."

"What do you do for a living, if I can ask?"

"I'm a potter. How about that?"

"I didn't think there was any money in it."

"There is when you make cheap souvenirs for the tourists," she said, and shrugged again. "Well—do you have any more questions about Walt Paige?"

"Not directly," I answered. "Did your brother know Paige very well?"

She seemed to tense slightly, but I could not be sure in the room's lighting. "About as well as I did, I suppose."

"Do you think he might know anything that would help?"

"I doubt it."

"Is he here now?"

"No, he went out earlier today. I can ask him about Walt when he gets home, and have him call you if he can help by some chance."

"I won't be pursuing things much further—as a matter of fact, I'll probably be returning to San Francisco tonight—so you'd better have him call Chief Quartermain at the City Hall."

"All right."

"One last thing, Beverly. Do you know a short, bald guy in his forties, dark and heavy-featured?"

"That doesn't sound like anybody I know. Why?"

"Paige talked with him not long before he was killed."

"A stranger in Cypress Bay?"

"There's no way of knowing just yet," I said. I got up on my feet. "I guess that's about all, Beverly. Thanks for your time and cooperation."

"Not at all."

She smiled and rose, and she was standing close enough to me so that I could look into her eyes. There was nothing there for me; I had simply not registered with her. So we went to the door and I did not say any of the tentative things a man says to a woman who appeals to him. But maybe it was just as well, I thought. She would not want another loveless affair, a man who had an itch to scratch, a man who was thinking of her only as pure sweet hell in bed; and I had absolutely nothing to offer her along any other lines.

We said goodbye on the porch and touched hands very briefly, and I went down the slab-stone steps without looking back at her. Bonificacio Drive was empty and quiet, like a street in Old Monterey when the air and the land and the sea were clean and you could take your time about living—and the to-morrows were all filled with promise.

Nine

The Cypress Point estate belonging to Robin and Jason Lomax was located on Inspiration Way, and I decided to make that my next stop. I took my car down to Ocean Boulevard and along to where it swung sharply to the east and became San Lucas Avenue. From there I could see Cypress Point—thickly wooded, rolling, moneyed acreage—extending into the aquamarine Pacific to form the southern boundary of the bay. Inspiration Way, according to my map, was a short street like the cross bar of an A, running north to south between two large drives that intersected out on the tip of the point. I turned off San Lucas and found it all right, and the Lomax estate came up on the left midway along.

One of those old-fashioned black-iron fences that look like connected rows of upright spears stretched away on both sides of a meandering entrance lane; the iron gates which normally would bar admittance to the grounds were standing open. I turned in and followed the lane through half an acre of moss-laced pine and carefully arranged ferns and rock terracing and miniature stone waterfalls that fed into glistening water-lilied pools. You half expected to see naiads and wood sprites cavorting in the ribbons of sunlight filtering through the tree branches. A Disney-world, created for fanciful children—or for nostalgic adults.

The drive leveled out finally on the floor of a tiny valley, with a solid wall of pine gently inclined to the rear and around on the left. The house was situated in the middle of the glen—a sprawling, modern, country-style home constructed of redwood and fieldstone, adorned by long eaves and high chimneys and old-bronze fittings. There was a flagstone terrace enclosed by moss-covered stone walls at the right, and beyond that more of the storybook landscaping; on the other side I could see a mesh-screened tennis court, floored in a thin layer of reddish-brown loam. A man and a woman were working a new tennis ball back and forth across a chain-link net, with the kind of fluid ease that comes from long practice and a genuine enthusiasm for the game. They were both dressed in solid white—the man in shorts and an Italian knit pullover; the woman in a short pleated tennis skirt and a sleeveless blouse—and they made a sharp contrast against the burnt-sienna color of the court, the dark greens and browns of the pines of the glade slopes.

I parked my car in front of the terrace wall, next to a new forest-green Mercedes. As I got out, a dark-haired little boy of five or six, wearing dungarees and a striped T-shirt, came running across the terrace and jumped up onto the moss-topped wall. He said "Hi!" exuberantly.

"Hi, guy."

"I've got a pet rabbit. Want to see him?"

"Well, maybe a little later."

"My name's Tommy Lomax. What's yours?"

I told him.

"My rabbit's name is Bugs," he said. He jumped down off the wall. "I'm feeding him carrots."

"Good for you."

He gave me a gap-toothed grin and ran back across the terrace again. I watched him out of sight, and then I turned, smiling a little, and followed a flagstone path through a facing rock-and-lady-fern garden, toward the tennis court.

The couple had stopped playing now and had come over to stand by the entrance to the enclosure. The guy had his racket turned horizontally, and he was bouncing the fuzzy white ball up and down on it like one of those rubber-band-and-rubber-ball paddle sets you used to see the kids playing with. He was about thirty-five, I saw as I approached, lean and trim and athletic and tanned; he wore a neatly barbered mustache, of the same rust-brown color as his razor-cut hair, and he had a Kirk Douglas cleft in the middle of his chin and an expression of mild curiosity on the good-natured mouth above it. The woman stood relaxed, arms down at her sides. Pale-gold hair—lighter than Judith Paige's, pulled into a horsetail and tied with a white ribbon—accentuated features as tanned as the guy's: button nose, quiet blue eyes, the kind of soft, small mouth that would smile often. She was very slim, with narrow hips, long coltish legs, apple-shaped breasts. They made a nice couple, standing there like that: health and perpetual youth, clean bodies and clean minds.

The woman said, "Hello," and smiled questioningly at me as I stepped up to the gate entrance.

"Mr. and Mrs. Lomax?"

"Yes," the guy said. "I don't believe we've had the pleasure?"

"No, we haven't." I introduced myself, and waited—but neither of them seemed to recognize my name; it was possible that they had not heard about Paige's death or about the small part I had played in it. I went on, "I have your name from Russell Dancer."

"Oh—really?" she said. There was no warmth, no feeling of any kind in her tone; apparently she had no fond memories about Russ Dancer or her days as a member of the laughter-and-liquor group. Maybe she thought guys like Dancer were beneath her now—or maybe I was just overreacting. "Are you a friend of Mr. Dancer's?"

"In a way," I said. "The reason I'm here has to do with a mutual acquaintance of yours and his, several years ago. A man named Walter Paige."

She jerked as if I had slapped her, and her color dissolved suddenly and completely under the tan. Lomax lost his polite smile and his eyes turned brittle and angry and his mouth pinched white at the corners. They stood staring at me, and it was abruptly very quiet in the small Disney valley; even the birds that had been singing soft medleys in the surrounding woods seemed breathlessly still. You could feel the sudden tension like a dark, chill wind.

Lomax said in a thin, tight voice, "Who the hell are you? What do you want here?"

"I'm a private detective. I'd like to—"

"Oh God!" Robin Lomax said.

She sounded stricken, and her husband put his arm around her and hated me too passionately with his eyes. "So that's the way it is," he said.

"The way what is, Mr. Lomax?"

"Get off my property."

"Just like that?"

"Just like that."

"Why?"

"Damn you, if you don't leave, I'll call the police."

"Maybe you'd better do that, Mr. Lomax," I said quietly. "I was at City Hall not long ago, but Chief Quartermain was out. He might have come back by now. You can tell him I'm here, if so, and you can tell him *why* I'm here. I think he'll be interested."

Some of the volatile anger went out of his eyes. He looked at

80

his wife for a long moment, and then the two of them looked at me again. "Why should Chief Quartermain be interested?" Lomax asked.

"You don't know?"

"No. Look, just why are you here?"

"I want to ask you some questions about Walter Paige."

"What's your involvement with Paige?"

"I found his body, for one thing."

"His . . . body?"

"That's right."

"He's dead?"

"He was murdered last night."

Deepening silence. They looked at each other again, but I could not read what passed between them—if anything passed between them. A muscle jumped on Lomax's left cheek, but there was nothing on his face or in his eyes that told me much. There was nothing in Robin Lomax's expression either as she stepped out of the half-circle of his arm, and the sighing breath she took might have meant anything at all.

"Who . . . killed him?" she asked softly.

"No one knows yet."

"Where did it happen?"

"In Cypress Bay. The Beachwood motel."

Lomax said, "Why was he back in Cypress Bay?"

"To meet a woman—and possibly for some other reason as well. He'd been coming here for the past five weekends."

"What woman? Someone from this area?"

"It would seem that way. She was with him shortly before he died."

Lomax wet his lips. "And what time was that?"

"Between five-thirty and quarter of six."

"You think we know something about it, is that it?"

"I didn't say that, Mr. Lomax."

"Well, we don't know anything about it. Robin and I were right here all of yesterday. We played tennis from midafternoon until dusk."

"Yes," she said. "Yes, that's right."

I studied their faces and I had the feeling that they were both lying, but it was Quartermain's place and not mine to break them down on it. I said, "What can you tell me about *The Dead and the Dying*?"

I had dragged that one out of left field, but it did not get me anything. Lomax looked surprised, and his wife still had that pale, stricken, withdrawn look about her. He said, "The what?"

"It's an old book of Russ Dancer's. Paige had a copy of it in his overnight bag. Do you know the book?"

"Hardly. We don't read the kind of trash Dancer writes."

Trash, I thought. A man's livelihood, a man's talent no matter how limited, a man's thoughts and feelings and impressions and guts. Trash. I said, "You didn't know that Paige had returned to Cypress Bay, I take it."

"Of course not. How would we know?"

"Mrs. Lomax?"

"No," she said. "No."

"He didn't try to contact you at any time?"

"Why should he contact me?"

"You didn't know him well originally?"

"No. I never cared to know him well."

"Why not?"

"He was vain and . . . crude."

"Who *did* know him well?"

"I have no idea."

"You were a regular member of the group, Mrs. Lomax."

"The affairs of others are no concern of mine," she said. "I never gave a thought to Walter Paige then, and I haven't since."

"Then why were you so upset when I first mentioned his name?"

82

Her mouth worked soundlessly for a moment, and she clutched at her husband's arm and put her eyes imploringly on his face. Lomax said with tremulous anger, "Listen, we don't have to talk to you any longer. You're not the police."

"The police will ask the same questions, Mr. Lomax."

"I don't care about that. Now get off my property."

"All right," I said. "But if I were you, I'd be a little more candid with Chief Quartermain than you've been with me. Innocent people don't need to lie or evade the truth."

I turned and left them standing there—a pair of bronzed statues with the beginnings of what might be an irremovable and no longer concealable tarnish marring their clean, polished luster. When I reached my car I could hear the little boy with the pet rabbit named Bugs, laughing happily from somewhere behind the house. The back of my neck felt cold. And as I drove out of there, the shaded areas on the landscaped grounds seemed deeper and darker, like shadowed corners hiding secret things.

Most of the shops along Grove Avenue were open to accommodate the Sunday tourist trade, and the sidewalks flowed with shoppers and strollers; vehicular traffic was heavy as well, and they had the traffic lights at the intersections and pedestrian crossings in operation. I crawled east toward Highway 1 and the Carmel Valley Road that would take me to Del Lobos Canyon, where the realtor, Keith Tarrant, lived.

The light at one of the pedestrian crossings about halfway along flashed red, and I stopped back of the crosswalk and took the time to put a cigarette into my mouth. I cupped my hands around the flame of the match, glancing over them and through the open window the way you do—and I saw the old faded-blue Studebaker pull to the curb on the other side of Grove Avenue. The passenger door opened immediately and a guy on that side got out, leaving the driver alone in the car. He stood on the sidewalk for a moment, face turned toward me, and I forgot the cigarette and the burning match.

It was the bald man I had seen with Walter Paige the previous afternoon.

I stared over at him, and he pivoted and moved away swiftly along Sierra Verde—one of Cypress Bay's quaint, winding village streets, and one that ended or began at Grove Avenue on that side. I felt the heat of the match then and dropped it on the floor and looked over to my right for a place to park; there was no opening. The traffic light had gone to green when I turned back again, and an impatient horn sounded behind me. I could not make a left turn across the narrow pedestrian walk that formed a break in the center divider; the only damned thing I could do was to go up to the next full intersection and negotiate a U-turn.

I got the car in gear and leaned on the gas trying to watch the street in front and the bald guy behind me on Sierra Verde. But it was no good. I lost sight of him before I had gone fifty feet, although I could still see the old Studebaker waiting at the curbing for a break in the steady stream of traffic moving down toward Ocean Boulevard. I tried to read the license number, but the angle was no good for that either; and all I had seen of the driver was a dark masculine head in quarter profile.

When I reached the intersection I could not complete the U-turn immediately because of the flow of cars, and I was forced to wait for the light. Half turned as I was, I could see the Studebaker wedge its way into the stream, but I still could not read the license number. The light changed finally and I made the turn and got down to Sierra Verde, working the brakes as I came abreast of the intersection. There was no sign of the bald guy; the sidewalks were less crowded along there, and if he had been walking in either of the first two blocks, I would have seen him.

My first impulse was to turn into Sierra Verde and try to locate him, but he might have gone anywhere—into one of the buildings, down an alleyway, onto a cross street—and if I turned up a blank it would be a complete one. The Studebaker was something else again. I could see it plainly enough two blocks down, stopped at a light. I made my decision, right or wrong, and followed Grove Avenue into the next block as the Stude moved with the changing light.

It was three cars in front of me when it made the turn north on Carmelo, one street up from Ocean Boulevard, and went out toward the Seventeen Mile Drive that took you on a scenic tour of Pebble Beach and Pacific Grove and the Monterey Peninsula. But the guy in the Studebaker was not going out on the drive. He stopped two blocks short of it, in front of a log-façaded tavern called the Stillwater, and hurried inside. I had a pretty good glimpse of him then; he was thirty or so, thick-shouldered, with dark hair wind-tossed and hanging down over his eyes; he wore brown slacks and a navy-blue windbreaker.

I parked close enough to see the Studebaker's license plate clearly, and copied the number down in my notebook; then I lit the cigarette that was still between my lips and waited with the engine running. I would give him ten minutes, I thought, and if he did not come out, I would go in after him. But it did not come to that; he was out in four and a half minutes, carrying something that might have been a quart bottle wrapped in a paper bag. He got into the Stude again and went down to the next corner and turned right and began to double back toward the center of Cypress Bay. I let him have two full blocks all the way.

He took me over to Guadalupe, and then east onto Mission Court, and then south on Santa Rosa. He made one more turn, east again, and drove half a block and took the Stude in to the curb. Then he slid out, carrying the paper-wrapped bottle, and went up twenty-five or thirty slab-stone steps, and, using a key, entered the Old Spanish adobe house with the rust-tile roof and the second-floor gallery and the tired reddish bougainvillaea growing over the short arbor at the top of the steps.

Bonificacio Drive.

The Winestock house.

And, very probably, Brad Winestock.

I drove past on the still quiet, still empty street, and made directly for the City Hall. The back of my neck had begun to feel cold again. The Lomaxes were hiding something, in spite of their denials and in spite of what Beverly Winestock had told me about Robin's noninvolvement with Paige; and even though Beverly herself had been cooperative, I had sensed an uneasiness in her, a holding back of something intangible—and since she had known about Paige's death for some time, whereas the Lomaxes apparently had not, she had had more time to prepare herself for possible questioning. Now there was her brother, linked to the bald man, who in turn had been linked to Walter Paige, and maybe she had been lying about the bald guy and about some of the other things as well.

You could feel the undercurrents lying blackly under the surface of it all, deep and swift, and you wondered where the bald man came into it and where the others came into it and who else might still come into it. You wondered how Russ Dancer's book worked into the scheme of things, if it worked in, and if Dancer had maybe been holding back something, too, for some reason of his own. And you wondered how far the undercurrents extended, and whether or not they formed a kind of intricate pattern, and just how deep and black they really were . . .

Ten

Quartermain was still in Salinas, and the fat sergeant still did not know when he would be back.

I stood looking at him and debating whether or not I should give him what I had learned thus far. I decided again that it should go directly to Quartermain, because the telling would take a while and Quartermain was patient and a good, careful listener; and, too, because I thought Quartermain would understand my own unauthorized involvement a little better. I told the sergeant the same thing I had earlier—that I would be back—and I went out to my car.

It was coming on late afternoon now, and I had not eaten anything all day. I stopped at the first café I saw and had coffee and a cheeseburger, and came to the conclusion that I would not be wise to confront Brad Winestock on my own. All I could justify in my own mind was the laying of a little groundwork, and if Winestock was directly involved in Paige's death, he could be dangerous. More important, I could conceivably do more harm than good with an unofficial visit—put him on his guard, perhaps even set him on the run if his involvement was deep enough. Quartermain was the one to talk to Winestock, all right; but I saw no harm in carrying out my previous intention of seeing Keith Tarrant and perhaps finding out a little more about those undercurrents which had been created by the catalyst, Walter Paige.

I went over to Highway 1 and south to Carmel Valley Road; Del Lobos Canyon was five miles in, judging from the map scale, and on the northern side. I drove into the valley and pretty soon I could see the lazy silver-blue path of the Carmel River, flanked by sycamore and willow trees—and pale-green artichoke fields and strawberry patches, and the well-known Carmel Valley pear orchards with their fragrant white spring blossoms like high, soft drifts of sun-bright snow. Cattle still grazed peacefully on the sloping sides of the valley, the way they had when the California rancheros led their quiet and languid lives on the fertile fields and flowing meadows that comprised the old Spanish land grants.

Del Lobos Canyon Road was narrow and wound upward along the side of the ravine itself; lichen-coated fence posts lined both sides, and on the left there were towering redwoods and moss-shawled oaks and an occasional home set high among the trees. Down in the canyon you could see flaming poison oak and sycamores and long multicolored carpets of wildflowers.

I came around a sharp bend, and ahead on my right—a hundred yards or so off the road—was one of these modern architectural wonders built in tiers at the edge of the canyon and a short distance down the sloping wall. The upper level of the house had a rear balcony that protruded above the second tier and its wider balcony, which in turn looked down on a deep, squarish brick terrace leaning out over the ravine on heavy steel girders. The construction materials were predominately red-wood and brick, with a lot of glass that caught the rays of late-afternoon sunlight and transformed them into burning, flame-tinged reflections, like demon eyes radiating images of an Old Testament hell.

I could see most of the terrace from the road, and it looked to be occupied by at least one person. It was the kind of day for sitting on your terrace, if you happened to have one. I drove a little further along and came to an unpaved connecting drive; at the head of it was an unobtrusive metal-on-wood sign that said: *Keith Tarrant—Realtor.* I turned in. The drive itself was shaded with thick-branched walnut trees, and a Japanese gardener had worked up a kind of bonzai garden with dwarf cypress in the fronting yard.

A large two-car port, attached to the side of the house, contained a cream-colored Chrysler Imperial and a sleek powder-blue Lotus; as I neared there, I saw that a winding series of steps had been cut out of the upper canyon wall, beyond the port, and that they led down toward the terrace. I parked to one side, in front of a second unobtrusive sign reiterating the fact that Keith Tarrant was a realtor, and walked over to the cut-out steps and looked down and around at the terrace. A man was standing at the front railing—a plump, light-haired guy with something that looked like a highball glass in his hand.

I went down the steps to where a narrow cut-out path, railed in redwood like the balconies and the terrace, led over to the second-tier platform. "Hello!" I called out to him. "Is it all right if I come down?"

He turned to look up at me, and then came away from the railing and took several steps across the brick flooring. He was smiling loosely. "Business or pleasure?" he asked, and his voice had a mild whiskey edge to it. It was that kind of day, too.

"Business, Mr. Tarrant," I told him, "but nothing to do with real estate, I'm afraid."

"Well, come ahead anyway."

I made my way down to the terrace and stepped through a kind of gate in the side railing and onto the smooth bricks. Tarrant came up to me, and I saw then that he only gave the impression of being plump, that he was not overweight at all. He had a round, convivial face and pale-brown hair thinning across the crown and a nice, easy, precise way of using his hands. He wore a pair of chino slacks and a dark-brown sports shirt and brown loafers, and there was just enough shine in his gray eyes to confirm the whiskey lilt in his voice. I thought that he was probably coming up on forty.

He said, "What can I do for you, Mr.—?"

I told him my name, but there was no immediate reaction. I said then, "I'm here about a man named Walter Paige, Mr. Tarrant; he was killed in Cypress Bay last night."

Tarrant blinked at me, and frowned, and then the furrows smoothed on his brow and he said, "Oh, you're the private detective, the one that found Paige at the motel."

"Yes."

"We heard about it on the radio this morning. Are you working with Chief Quartermain on the investigation?"

"Not exactly. This is an unofficial visit, more or less."

"I see. Well—what brings you to me?"

"I understand you knew Paige at one time."

"Unfortunately, yes. How did you discover that?"

"From Russ Dancer."

"Oh? And what led you to him?"

"Paige had one of Dancer's books at the motel," I said. "A paperback, published in 1954, called *The Dead and the Dying*. Do you know it, Mr. Tarrant?"

He shook his head. "I don't have much time to read, and I don't usually go in for the kind of things Russ Dancer writes, anyway. Why would Paige have a copy of one of Russ's old books?"

"That's a question that has no answer just yet."

"Doesn't Dancer have any idea?"

"No, he doesn't."

"That's rather odd about the book," Tarrant said. "I can't imagine Paige being interested in anything of Dancer's; the two of them never got along."

90

"You mean there was hostility between them?"

"I suppose you could say that."

"What was the cause of it?"

"I don't remember exactly."

"A woman?"

"It might have been."

"Was it an open hostility?"

"How do you mean?"

"Did they have words, something more maybe?"

"Words, I guess. It's pretty hazy in my mind. Why don't you ask Russ about it?"

"I'll do that—or the police will."

Tarrant gave me his loose smile. "How about a drink? I could stand another one."

"I don't think so, thanks."

He shrugged and drained what was left in the highball glass. "I'll fill up again, if you don't mind. Sunday is the only day I get to relax, and I always manage to relax a little better with a few drinks inside me."

"Sure," I said.

He turned and crossed to the overhang of the second-tier balcony and under it and through an open sliding-glass panel, into a lounge or game room. I had a glimpse of a long bleached-mahogany bar and a couple of ivory-leather stools and what appeared to be a felt-topped card table. I walked over to the terrace railing, in front of an arrangement of patio furniture, and put my hands on the redwood planking and looked over and down. It was a long way into the oak-floored canyon below. I had never been much for heights, and I stepped back a little and gazed across the gap at a lupine- and poppy-strewn meadow that stretched from the top of the ravine wall toward the horizon. It did not quite make it; chaparral and pine took over, and leaned up to touch the white-streaked blue of the heavens.

Tarrant came back after a time, with a full glass, and I said,

"Nice view you've got," because it was the thing to say—and because it was.

"The finest in the valley, for my money," he agreed. "That's why I saved it for myself."

"Do you operate your realty office from here?" I asked him. "I noticed the signs out front."

"Mostly. I keep a small office and a secretary in Cypress Bay, of course." He had some of his fresh drink. "Was there anything specific you wanted to know about Walt Paige—or just general impressions? I really don't know much about him."

"Well, were you surprised to learn of his return to this area?"

"Surprised and not at all pleased. I never particularly liked him, to be frank. He was arrogant and overbearing, and we were hardly more than civil to one another."

There was something in the way he said it that made me ask, "Was this morning's radio report the first you knew of his return?"

"No. He made a local call to me here, four or five weekends ago."

"For what reason?"

"He wanted to rent a piece of property in Cypress Bay that I happened to be handling."

I frowned. "Real estate or a private home?"

"Neither. A small vacant shop on Balboa, off Grove."

"What sort of shop?"

"It was formerly a newsstand," Tarrant said. "The previous owner had gone out of business the week before, due to a lack of funds and some hard luck with vandals."

"Did you rent the shop to Paige?"

"No."

"Why not?"

"To put it simply, I didn't like the idea of him settling in Cy-

92

press Bay; he wasn't the kind of man you like to see in your community. So I refused rental to him."

"How did he react to that?"

"He didn't like it, naturally."

"Was he abusive?"

"Not really. He tried to talk me into reconsidering, but when he realized I wasn't having any, he broke the connection."

"Did you hear from him again?"

"That was the one and only time."

"Is the shop still unrented?"

Tarrant moved his head negatively. "Central store property in Cypress Bay is in heavy demand, and I've never had any problem renting vacancies; that's why I could afford to refuse to do business with Paige. I rented the shop two days later, to a party from Los Angeles."

"Did Paige tell you why he wanted it?"

"He said he had come into a small amount of money, and had always liked Cypress Bay, and was interested in going into business there. He didn't say what sort of business, but I assumed it was another newsstand that he had in mind; the shop is too small for much else."

I tried to make something out of all this, and made nothing at all. I said, "Do you know if he contacted anyone of a mutual acquaintance while he was in Cypress Bay the past five weekends?"

"Such as who?"

"Russ Dancer, Robin Lomax, either of the Winestocks."

"Not to my knowledge, no."

"Paige had been seeing a woman during these weekend visits of his," I said. "It's possible she was one he knew when he lived here previously. Any idea who she might be?"

"He had quite a string of conquests to his credit, from what I gathered," Tarrant said. "I never knew what any of them saw in him. How do you know he was seeing a woman in Cypress Bay?"

"There were indications."

"Indications?"

"Facts that haven't been made public."

"Oh—I see. No, I don't know who she might be. Do the police think she killed him?"

"There's the chance of it."

"And they have no clues to her identity?"

"Not at the moment, anyway."

"Frankly, I hope they never find out," Tarrant said. "If she killed Paige, she did the world something of a favor." He had a little more of his drink. "You were working for Paige's young wife, according to the radio. Divorce evidence?"

"In a way."

"That's ironic, isn't it?"

"I guess you could say that."

"How is she taking his death?"

"Badly."

"She'll get over it. Women are adaptable creatures."

"Yeah," I said. "Look, Mr. Tarrant, do you know a dark, balding man, about forty, wedge-shaped and heavy-featured? He may be a friend of Brad Winestock's."

Tarrant frowned thoughtfully. "No, I don't think so. I haven't seen Winestock in some time—we don't move in the same circles any longer—and I wouldn't know any of his current friends. Why do you ask?"

"Paige met this man shortly before he was killed," I said. "The police would like to know who he is and why he had his meeting with Paige."

"I see."

I said, "Well, I won't bother you any longer, Mr. Tarrant. I appreciate your talking to me."

94

"Glad to do it," he said. He got a wallet from the rear pocket of his chinos. "Let me give you a couple of my business cards, in the event you or your friends are ever in the market for real estate in this area."

I wanted to tell him it was not likely that I or any present or future friends of mine would ever be in the market for property in Cypress Bay and environs, but I said nothing. I let him give me three small white embossed cards and tucked them away in my own wallet. We shook hands, and he raised his glass to me in a congenial parting and turned away to look down into the canyon as I crossed the terrace to the side railing.

When I reached the top of the cut-out steps, I paused to light a cigarette; then I shook the match out and put it under the cellophane wrapping on the Pall Mall package and started over to my car. Just as I got there, the front door of the house opened and an auburn-haired woman wearing a yellow sundress came outside. She stood for a moment, looking at me uncertainly, and then she came forward and around the car to where I was standing.

She was a few years younger than Tarrant, tall and golden and lithe—not beautiful, but possessed of a certain intangible beauty nonetheless. A dusting of tiny sepia-colored freckles adorned the bridge of her nose, and she had a wide, mobile mouth and eyes that were very pale except for a violet-blue rim about the irises. The auburn hair was cut semi-long; she wore it waved, with long bangs to partially conceal a high forehead. Her body was strong and nice, and the yellow sundress, low at the bodice and high at the hem, let you see a good deal of it.

She said, "I'm Bianca Tarrant, Keith's wife," and smiled in a vague way. Her eyes had the same kind of shine that Tarrant's had had, and you could tell that he had not been drinking alone on this afternoon.

"How are you, Mrs. Tarrant?"

95

"I was down in the lounge," she said, "and I heard part of what you and my husband were talking about—enough to know who you are and why you're here."

I had nothing to say to that, so I smiled at her and waited politely.

She said, "Have you any idea who killed Walter Paige?"

"Not at the moment. The police are working on several possibilities."

"He was a good man," she said softly. "He didn't deserve to die the way he did."

"Did you know him well, Mrs. Tarrant?"

"We were good friends six years ago."

"Had you seen him since he returned to Cypress Bay?"

"No. No, I hadn't seen him. I didn't know he'd come back."

"And if you had?" I asked gently.

"What?"

"Would you have liked to see him again?"

"Yes," she answered, "yes, I would have liked to see him again." The pale eyes seemed depthless now. "I hope you find his killer. I hope you make him pay dearly for his crime."

She turned before I could say anything else, and walked quickly and somewhat unsteadily back to the house. The door clicked shut after her. I stood there by the car, looking at the closed door and listening to the soft voice of a late-afternoon breeze calling across the rim of the canyon—and thinking again about those deep and black and far-reaching undercurrents.

Eleven

I wedged my car into a parking space on Balboa Street and went over to look at the newsstand Walter Paige had attempted to rent.

It was still unoccupied and there was not much to see. It had a narrow adobe front with a padlock on the door, and an oblong facing window that was partially obscured by soaping and imprinted with the words *Martin's News Agency;* there was a sidewalk awning, but it had been rolled back above the door and window. The shop's immediate neighbor to the north was a combination candy store and soda fountain; to the south, a dark and cobblestoned little alley led eastward through the center of the block to Pine Street, and its opposite wall belonged to a curio shop. I was able to look inside the newsstand past the soaped glass, but there was nothing except shadowed emptiness. Apparently the new tenant had not as yet taken possession; or if he had, intended to renovate before moving in fresh stock and opening for business.

I went down the alley a little way, and the newsstand had a side door that showed signs of having been forcibly entered at one time—the vandals Tarrant had mentioned—and which now was also padlocked from the outside. I thought that it would open on a storeroom, since the building was considerably longer than it was wide and the interior I had glimpsed through the window was less than three-quarters of the overall length. The rear wall of the structure was set flush with the rear wall of another building facing on Pine Street; just for the hell of it I went through to Pine and looked at the storefront there, and it was a mod boutique that specialized in hand-tooled leather garments for men and women "of discerning taste."

There was nothing in any of this that I could see. Maybe Paige had had the honest intention of opening a small newsstand in Cypress Bay, although that seemed pretty much out of character; or maybe he had had some ulterior motive that I could not even begin to interpret; or maybe Tarrant had been lying about Paige's call for some reason of his own.

More things to wonder about, I thought—too many things. The Lomaxes and the Winestocks and the balding guy and what Russ Dancer had not told me about his relationship with Walter Paige and just what Bianca Tarrant's relationship had been with Walter Paige and whether or not Keith Tarrant had been completely honest and why Paige had tried to rent a vacant store in downtown Cypress Bay. And Dancer's damned book, *The Dead and the Dying*, and why Paige had had it and just what it meant, if it meant anything at all . . .

I returned to Balboa Street and got into my car and started for the City Hall again. But I had to pass near the Bay Head Inn to get there, and I decided it was about time I looked in again on Judith Paige. I felt vaguely guilty about neglecting to check on her since the morning; it was not healthy for her to sit up in that dark room alone, grieving, perhaps brooding, and I wanted to make sure everything was all right.

I parked in front of the place and went inside and up the curving staircase to the second floor. She opened the door herself this time, in response to my knock, and she looked considerably better than she had earlier. She had put a touch of coral lipstick on her mouth and brushed her hair a little, and the wistfulness and the sorrow were tempered with a certain resolve. I felt myself relax, looking at her. She was going to be okay now; you could tell it by her eyes and by the way she carried herself.

I said, "Hello, Mrs. Paige. I just thought I'd stop by to see how you were feeling."

"Much better, thank you," she said, and gave me a small, brave smile.

"Have you been alone here all day?"

"Well, Chief Quartermain came by twice—once this morning, after you left, and once a little while ago."

"That's good. How about food? Have you eaten?"

"We went for a walk, and he bought me some soup and a sandwich. I didn't think I wanted to go out, or to eat anything, but now I'm glad I did."

So am I, I thought. "Did the Chief have any . . . news?"

"No, I don't think so. He didn't say, if he had."

And I was not going to say either, not at this point. There were too many intangibles, for one thing, and for another she was starting to bear up fine now and the kind of facts I did know for certain could only have upset her. I said, "Did he tell you whether or not we—you—could leave for San Francisco tonight?"

"Yes. He said it was all right."

"Good. I've got to go over to see him now, and there's the chance I'll have to stay on here for another day or so. If so, I'll call you and let you know—and I'm sure the Chief will assign someone to drive you to the airport in Monterey, and make arrangements for someone else to meet you in San Francisco and take you home."

"All right," she said. "But why should you have to stay here another day?"

"I'm not certain that I will have to; it just may work out that way." I paused. "If it does, would you mind if I called you in San Francisco when I get back? And maybe dropped out to see you?"

She had another of those small smiles for me. "No, of course I wouldn't mind. I think I'll need someone to talk to, until I can return to my family."

* We touched hands, and hers was soft and moist and very tiny in mine—a child's hand. Christ, she made me feel paternal. I resisted an impulse to kiss her cheek, smiled at her, and left her again with some regrets.

I drove on to City Hall, and this time Quartermain was there. The fat sergeant told me he had come in a half-hour earlier, apparently just after he had left Judith for the second time; the sergeant got a phone okay for me to go in, and buzzed open the electronic doors. Less than a minute later I opened the door to Quartermain's private office.

He was sitting behind the walnut desk with the heels of his hands pressed against his temples, as if he were suffering a savage headache. His sad face had a weary, houndish look. I shut the door quietly, and he said, "I would have been back two hours ago, but I stopped in at the Bay Head to see Mrs. Paige."

I sat down in the same armchair I had occupied that morning. "I know," I said. "I just left her myself."

"She seems to be holding her own now."

"I thought so too. It was good of you to take her out for a walk and something to eat."

"Yeah, well, she needed it," he said. He lowered his hands and swiveled around to look at me. "Donovan, out on the desk, said you'd stopped by twice to see me while I was gone. What's on your mind?"

"Quite a few things," I told him. "I've spent the day putting my nose into things, where it probably doesn't belong."

"Paige's death, you mean?"

"Yes."

100

"In what way?"

"Well, it started with the book."

"The paperback from Paige's bag?"

"Uh-huh. There was a lead in it after all."

"What sort of lead?"

"The author, Russell Dancer. I'd read some of his pulp stories, and they were set in the San Francisco area—the later ones; so was *The Dead and the Dying*. So I followed a hunch and looked him up in the local telephone directory."

"He's listed?"

"R. Dancer, Beach Road, County."

"Christ, I never even thought of that possibility."

"You can't think of everything," I said. "And you can't know everybody who lives in or around your community."

"I suppose not," he admitted. "I take it there was a connection between Dancer and Paige?"

I nodded. "Dancer knew him about six years ago."

"Where?"

"Cypress Bay. Paige lived here for six or seven months, and he was part of a bar-hopping group that included Dancer and several other local residents. He was apparently involved with most of them, in one way or another."

"How do you mean?"

"Like this," I said, and I told him the rest of it, slowly, including each of my impressions. He let me tell it once without interruption; then he had me repeat parts of it, asking questions now and then and making notes on a ruled pad. Finally he sat back and tapped the clip of his pen against his front teeth, but there was no disapproval for me on his long face. I thought it was going to keep on being all right between us.

He said, "I shouldn't have been so quick to discount that goddamned book; it seems to have keyed open a few local closets."

"I think it ties in further, too," I said, "but I can't figure how. I drew nothing but blanks when I asked about it."

"I don't like the way all this is shaping up," Quartermain said. "Last night Paige's death had most of the earmarks of a simple crime of passion, but you've uncovered a hell of a lot of potential complications and involvements. Murder in a town like Cypress Bay is bad enough, but when some of the more respected members of the community begin figuring into it, it's a damn sight worse. I know Keith Tarrant and the Lomaxes, and I'm not going to relish digging into their private lives—especially if it means a large amount of adverse publicity. We're a resort town, primarily, and we can't afford any kind of a major blow-off."

I did not say anything.

Quartermain made an abrupt deprecating gesture. "Hell, that sounds callous and insular, and those are two things I try not to be. I didn't mean that I intend to soft-pedal my investigation; I'm a cop and I've got a job to do and I'm going to do it the best way I know how—publicity or no publicity. I guess I was just thinking out loud, lamenting a little."

"Nobody likes to see a blow-off in his town," I said. "A cop least of all."

"Yeah," he said, and sighed. "Well, maybe those skeletons that seem to be rattling around don't include the bones of murder; that's something to hope for anyway."

"What are you going to do first, if I can ask?"

"Talk to Brad Winestock," he answered. "I want to know who this bald man is and why he keeps turning up."

"I'd like to know that myself."

He looked at me for a time, meditatively. "You want to tag along for the ride?"

I sat up straight in the chair. I had not expected anything like that; at best, I had figured him to ask me to hang around for another day or two. "Hell yes, if you'll have me."

102

"You've done a considerable amount of spadework, and I think that earns you the right to sit in—and to hell with the rule-book."

"Thanks, Chief."

"Ned—for God's sake." He got up on his feet. "I think it's a good idea if Mrs. Paige got out of here and back home; familiar surroundings are what she needs right now. Since you'll be staying on, I'll make arrangements for her to fly into San Francisco International from Monterey. You want to call her and tell her?"

"Yes."

"Use my phone. I'll go out and have Donovan set it up, here and in San Francisco."

I rang up Judith at the Bay Head Inn and told her that I was going to have to remain in Cypress Bay another day, after all, and that Quartermain was making preparations for her return by plane. She said that was fine, although she would have preferred driving back with me. There was a warm thing for me in those words, and I held onto it, down inside. I promised to call her as soon as I got home to San Francisco, or if anything came up that she ought to know. I also told her to keep away from television and radio broadcasts, and the newspapers, because they could only upset her—and not to talk to any reporters if they came around; she was better, but not quite ready to find out about her husband's infidelity or background or prison record, and the less she knew for a while, the stronger she would be when she finally had to face the whole truth. She agreed to do as I requested, and asked me to thank the Chief for his kindness, and we said a soft parting.

Quartermain came back, and it was all arranged. So we left his office then, without any more words, and went out to the police parking area and picked up his unmarked car—a couple of old firehorses who maybe thought too much about the problems of others and not enough about their own; who cared too much and expected too much, and perhaps could not have existed any other way. I had the idea that he sensed that bond, too, and that that was another part of the reason he had invited me to come along.

Cypress Bay: the town with a little something for everyone . . .

Twelve

The shadows on the porch beneath the second-floor gallery were deeper and cooler now, with the coming of night, and the faint fragrance of the red bougainvillaea was like the wistful memory of a sweetheart and a perfume of long ago. You could see the Pacific from up there—a burning sheet of glass under a fiery sun that was just touching the juncture of sea and sky to the west—and the full sweep of the heavens, where blue had modulated to gold-veined gray. Sunset, laying a golden veil over the land before giving way to the black curtain of night.

Beverly Winestock answered the melancholy chimes, as she had earlier in the day. She looked even more ephemeral now, silhouetted against the shadowed hall behind her, and her dark hair was the same dusky, flowing tapestry; she was still sensual, still desirable, but there was a tenseness in her now, a strain that seemed to rob her of some of her beauty. Her eyes touched my face and moved away, leaving nothing; she looked at Quartermain, waiting, silent.

He introduced himself and showed her his identification and asked her, "Is your brother home at the moment, Miss Winestock?"

She looked past him, down along the slab-stone steps and

beyond the front gate to where the faded-blue Studebaker was parked on Bonificacio Drive—to Quartermain's car parked behind it. Then she looked at me again, tight-lipped, and said to Quartermain, "Yes, he's here."

"We'd like to see him, please."

"What about?"

"We'll discuss that with him, if you don't mind."

She hesitated a moment longer, and then shrugged and put her back to us and walked away along the hall. Quartermain and I went inside, and I shut the door. Beverly stopped at the entrance to the tile-floored parlor and half turned back to us.

A man's voice called from within, "Who is it, Bev?"

She did not answer. When Quartermain and I approached, she turned again and disappeared through the arch at the far end of the hall. I watched her for a moment before I followed Quartermain into the parlor, thinking: She's got a wall up now, a protective barrier—cool and aloof and a million miles away. It was down earlier, when I was here, but she's put it back up, and with that tenseness in her it can only mean there's a threat of some kind, to her or to her brother . . .

Brad Winestock was sitting on the tapestried-cloth sofa, his arms resting forward on his knees; he still wore the brown slacks of the afternoon, and his dark hair was still wind-tangled, but he had shed the blue windbreaker to reveal a ribbed short-sleeved pullover cord-laced from mid-chest to throat in one of the current casual fashions. There was a quart of Jim Beam on the brass-ornamented table in front of him, down about six inches, and an empty glass beside it. I thought that it was probably the bottle he had bought at the Stillwater, and that he had been working on it ever since he had gotten home.

He said, "Yeah? What is it?"

His voice was thick, and his eyes—a flat brown with too much white showing—were hazy and restless. There was a thin film of sweat on his forehead. Quartermain glanced at me, and I

106

nodded slightly to confirm that this was the man who had been with the balding guy, the man I had followed here from Grove Avenue.

He stepped forward and said to Winestock, "My name is Quartermain—the Chief of Police of Cypress Bay. I'd like to ask you a few questions."

Winestock seemed to stiffen slightly, and his eyes were furtive things that touched this and that in the room without focusing on anything at all. He was nervous and he was somewhat afraid, and you could see that the last man on earth he wanted to have in his living room was the local Chief of Police.

"What questions?" he asked heavily. "What about? I haven't done anything."

"Nobody said you had," Quartermain told him.

"What do you want, then?"

"I understand you knew a man named Walter Paige at one time."

Winestock opened his mouth and wet his lips the way a man who has been drinking will do. "Yeah," he said. "Yeah, I knew him once."

"You know he's dead, of course."

"It was on the radio."

"When was the last time you saw him?"

"Hell, I don't know. Six or seven years."

"You didn't know he'd returned to Cypress Bay?"

"No, I never knew it."

"Who do you suppose killed him?"

"How would I know who?"

"Are you aware of any enemies he might have had?"

"Walt was a good guy, he didn't have enemies."

"I thought you hadn't seen him in six or seven years."

"Six or seven years ago, I meant. He didn't have any enemies then." Winestock's eyes jerked away from Quartermain and moved over me like fevered hands. "You're the guy that came around here bothering Bev today, the one who found Walt."

"That's right," I said.

"She doesn't know anything," Winestock said. "What do you want to bother her for?"

"What do *you* know, Winestock?" Quartermain asked him.

"Nothing. Why should I know anything?"

Quartermain went over and sat down on one of the chairs; I remained where I was, not far from the door. To Winestock he said, "Would you tell us where you were today?"

"Today? Why?"

"Just answer the question."

"I was right here, mostly."

"But you did go out, is that right?"

"Yeah, for a little while."

"To where?"

"For a drive. Just for a drive."

"Where did you go on this drive?"

"Down the coast. To Big Sur."

"Alone?"

"Why? What difference does that make?"

"Were you alone, Winestock?"

"Yeah, for Christ's sake, I was alone!"

"All right," Quartermain said quietly, "tell me about the bald man—the one who was seen getting out of your car on the corner of Grove and Sierra Verde earlier this afternoon."

Winestock blinked rapidly three times, and his hands went out in a convulsive movement toward the bottle and glass on the table; but the hands were spasmodic and he seemed to have lost control of them momentarily. The glass tipped over and fell off the table and rolled under the sofa. He said "Shit!" in a thin voice and sat back and folded his arms tightly across his chest.

"Well?" Quartermain asked.

Winestock hesitated, and you could watch him searching

for an answer. Then: "A hitchhiker. A hitchhiker I picked up down the coast. I didn't even think about him before." Pause. "Listen, why are you interested in him?"

"Hitchhiker," Quartermain said.

"That's right."

"You in the habit of picking up hitchhikers, are you?"

"Sometimes, what the hell."

"Tell us about this one."

"What about him?"

"Was he a stranger to you?"

"I never saw him before today."

"What was his name?"

"He didn't say."

"What *did* he say?"

"Nothing. We didn't talk much."

"Where was he headed for?"

"I don't know."

"What was he doing out on the highway?"

"I told you, we didn't talk much."

"Why did you let him out at Grove and Sierra Verde?"

"That's where he wanted to get out."

"Did he have business in Cypress Bay, in that area?"

"Goddamn it, I don't know!"

"You're sure you never saw him before?"

"How many times do I have to tell you?"

"He was a friend of Paige's, did you know that?"

"What? How do you——?"

"He was seen with Paige yesterday."

"I don't know anything about it."

"That's your story, then: a hitchhiker, a stranger."

"It's the truth," Winestock said. "I'm telling you."

"Where were you yesterday, say five-thirty P.M.?"

"Listen, now, I didn't have anything to do with Paige getting killed. I didn't have anything to do with that."

"Tell us where you were," Quartermain said patiently.

"Next door. Yeah, five-thirty, I was next door with Harry Jacobs." He looked somewhat relieved, although his face still shone with the bright sweat of fear. "Yeah, Harry and me were working on his cat."

"His what?"

"Catamaran, he's got this cat. We were working on it."

"Who else was there?"

"Harry's wife, she was there, she saw us."

Quartermain stood up. "Let's go talk to the Jacobses."

"Sure," Winestock agreed. "Sure, they'll tell you."

We went out through the rear of the house. There was no sign of Beverly, but I had the feeling she was somewhere close by, perhaps watching, perhaps listening. The rear yard was small and shaded by a pair of pepper trees, and there was a low redwood fence separating the Winestock property from a similar lot—and a similar Old Spanish house—next door.

Winestock stepped over the stake fence and led us along a narrow path to the rear door. He rapped loudly on the screen and called, "Harry! Hey, Harry, it's me, Brad!"

Pretty soon the door opened, and a guy about thirty—tanned, running to fat, wearing dungarees and a white sweat-shirt—looked out at us. Quartermain asked him if he was Harry Jacobs, and the guy said that he was—hello, Brad, who're your friends? Quartermain said that he was the Chief of Police and Jacobs looked surprised and puzzled, but hardly upset; he told us, readily enough, that sure, Brad had been with him yesterday afternoon around five-thirty, working on the cat, he'd had her out on the bay that morning and she—

"Did Winestock leave at any time between four and six?" Quartermain asked.

"No, he didn't leave until after dark."

"Is your wife home, Mr. Jacobs?"

"Sure. You want to talk to her?"

110

"If you wouldn't mind."

"Sure, sure. Hey, Angie, come here, will you?"

Angie was a faded blonde, tanned, also running to fat, wearing dungarees and a white sweatshirt; superficially at least, I thought, they were the ideal couple. She confirmed the fact that Winestock had been with her husband, working on their catamaran from about three the previous afternoon until after dark —and that Winestock had not left during that time.

"All right," Quartermain said, and thanked the two of them.

"Say, what's it all about?" Jacobs asked.

"Nothing, Harry, just a mistake," Winestock said, and laughed nervously.

Quartermain and I did not have anything to say. We returned to the Winestock house, and there was still no sign of Beverly. In the parlor again, Winestock retrieved his glass from under the sofa and poured himself a good hooker and had it off without taking a breath. Quartermain and I watched him dispassionately.

"What else can you tell us about Walter Paige?" Quartermain asked him finally.

"Nothing. It's been six or seven years, like I told you."

"How well did you know him back then?"

"Not well, just a few drinks here and there."

"He was pretty good with the women, wasn't he?"

"Oh sure, he always had the women."

"Like who, for instance?"

"A whole string, who knows exactly?"

"Was your sister a good friend of Paige's?"

"What the hell do you mean by that? Listen—"

"Answer the question, Winestock."

"No. No, she hardly knew him."

"You know Russ Dancer, don't you?"

"Yeah, I know him."

"How well did he and Paige get along?"

"All right, I guess."

"I've heard there was once some bad blood between them."

"I don't know anything about that."

"You're sure?"

"I'd tell you if I knew anything, Jesus Christ!"

"Did you ever read anything of Dancer's?"

Winestock wet his lips open-mouthed again. "Like what?"

"You tell me."

"I read a couple of his westerns, yeah."

"How about a book called *The Dead and the Dying*?"

"I never heard of it," Winestock said immediately. "Why do you want to know about that?"

"Why would Paige have a copy of it?"

"How the hell would I know? Listen, what do you want out of me, huh? I don't know anything about Paige, I don't know anything about a goddamn book. Why don't you leave me alone, a man's got the right to be left alone."

Quartermain watched him steadily for several long, silent seconds; his blue eyes were cold and sharp and calculating. Winestock kept his gaze averted, sweating, fidgeting. Finally Quartermain said, "I guess that's about all for now. But I might want to talk to you again, Winestock. You'll be available, won't you?"

"I'm not going anywhere. I haven't done anything."

"I hope that's true."

"It's true, all right." He wiped the back of his right hand across his damp forehead. "Look, I hope you get whoever killed Walt."

"We'll get him," Quartermain said. "Or her. Nobody is going to get away with murder in Cypress Bay."

Winestock was reaching for the bottle again, jerkily, as we stepped out of the parlor.

When Quartermain and I were sitting in his car on the street outside, he said, "You're probably wondering why I didn't pull him in—and why I didn't talk to the sister."

"Well, you wouldn't have gotten anything out of her. If she knows what it is that's making Winestock sweat, she'll guard hell out of it to protect him."

"Yeah. And as far as pulling Winestock in, his alibi seems okay for the time of Paige's death, at least for now, and I don't have much to hold him on; and I've got the feeling he did as much talking in there as he's going to do for the time being. But he'll sweat more now, wondering if and when we'll be back, and if he sweats long enough and hard enough, it might break this thing open."

"Giving him rope?"

"That's it. He knows that bald man, all right—and he knows more about Walter Paige than he's telling."

"Dancer's book, too," I said. "Did you notice how quick his denials were?"

"I noticed," Quartermain answered grimly.

He pulled away from the curb, and once we were on our way he called Donovan and asked him to contact Lieutenant Favor at his home. When Donovan had done that, and had Favor waiting on standby, Quartermain issued orders for immediate stakeout duty on the Winestock house, saying that we would maintain surveillance on the southwestern corner of Bonificacio and Los Robles until Favor's arrival. Through Donovan, the lieutenant said he would be there within twenty minutes.

We circled the block and parked, and from the corner we could see Winestock's Studebaker and anyone leaving or entering the Winestock house. I could see, too, a thin whitish muggers' moon in the purple-black night sky, and it seemed to have the look of a scythe blade hanging poised over Cypress Bay. Nightmare symbolism, I thought; the hell with that. But I

113

felt uneasy, keyed up—the same feeling you might have if you were standing on ground above a series of earth faults and you knew the faults were there and you could hear a distant rumbling and feel vague tremors beneath your feet. Something was going to happen, you sensed that, you knew the whole thing was going to crack wide open pretty soon now. And when it did, there would be tragedy and pain, and even if you escaped the immediacy of it yourself, the shock waves would reach you and touch you and just maybe they would hurt you a little too . . .

Thirteen

The faded-blue Studebaker was still sitting dark and empty on the street, and no one had come out of or gone into the Winestock house, when Favor arrived fifteen minutes later. If Brad Winestock was going somewhere tonight, it seemed he was in no hurry about it; either that, or he was being cautious.

Favor pulled up behind us, headlamps dark, and Quartermain got out briefly to talk to him; then he came back and started the car and turned south on Bonificacio. I said, "Where to now?"

He switched on the lights. "To have a talk with the Lomaxes, I think."

We drove out to Cypress Point, and the front gate on Inspiration Way was still open; but when we got down into the tiny valley, the Lomax house was void of lights and sound and the forest-green Mercedes was gone. Old-bronze night lamps were mounted on either side of the front door, and pole lights spaced at intervals encircled the mesh-screened tennis court, but these, too, were unlighted. The only illumination came from the moon, pale and ghostly.

We got out of the car and went up to the door, the way you have to do even though you know it's pointless. Quartermain

115

rang the bell, and chimes tolled emptily through the interior and faded into deep stillness again. We stood there for a couple of minutes, waiting for nothing at all, and then returned to the car.

Quartermain said, "Maybe they're out to dinner, or a movie."

"Maybe so. But why didn't they close the front gate then? Or put on the night-lighting?"

"That doesn't have to mean much."

"Just that they were in a hurry."

"People are always in a hurry," he said. "We'll come back later, or in the morning. They'll be home eventually."

"Do you know them well, Ned?"

"Well enough. I thought I did, anyway."

I had nothing to say to that. I fired another cigarette and coughed out the match and kept on coughing as he swung the car around onto the entrance lane. Too many cigarettes again today—Christ! The moss-laced pine and the rock terracing and the miniature waterfalls had a look of unreality about them in the darkness, as if they were papier-mâché imitations on some elaborate stage set. The feeling added depth and fuel to my continuing sense of uneasiness.

When we got to Inspiration Way, I asked, "Now where?"

"Russell Dancer."

"And then?"

"That depends on what Dancer has to say."

We drove down to Highway 1 and turned south. The sea was black and restless under a thin breeze, and the proud old cypress trees silhouetted against the night sky were like manifestations of the essence of loneliness. On the horizon, a mist had begun to form; it drifted slowly landward, vaguely luminous, a little eerie: a nameless something, an other-worldly substance reaching out to embrace the primordial landscape . . .

The urgent crackling of the transceiver set under the dash snapped me out of that sort of melodramatic reflecting. Quartermain caught up the handset immediately, and it was Lieutenant Favor to tell us Brad Winestock had just left his house and gotten into his car and was proceeding north on Bonificacio Drive. Favor was maintaining surveillance. Quartermain told him to keep reporting every thirty seconds until Winestock reached an ultimate destination; then he pulled the car into a turnout that came up on our right. He said to me, "Things are beginning to break."

"I thought they might."

"But I don't like it much. I've got a feeling."

I looked at him. "What kind of feeling?"

"Bad vibrations. Does that sound asinine?"

"No," I told him. "I've got them too."

He ran one of his big hands over his face. "We'll stay here until we find out where Winestock goes. If it looks like anything, we'll want to get there in a hurry."

Favor's voice said from the transceiver, "Subject proceeding east on Pescadero, toward Highway One."

Quartermain and I sat there listening to static and silence for another half-minute; then: "Subject turning north on Highway One. I'm approaching the intersection now . . . Oh Christ!"

Quartermain jabbed at the mike's *Send* button. "What's the matter?"

"There's a string of cars heading south," Favor said. "Winestock just beat them and I'm bottled up here . . ."

"Wedge out there, for God's sake!"

"I'm trying, Ned . . . Okay, here's a break . . . I'm turning now and I've got my foot into it; I can't see his taillights, but he can't have gotten far . . ."

Static. More static. Quartermain said urgently, "Jim? Do you see him?"

"No. Ned, there's no sign of him. The Carmel Highway turnoff is coming up, and he might have taken that. I've got to make a choice . . ." Static. "All right, I'm taking Carmel Highway. One looks clear . . ." Static. "Nothing, no sign of him . . ." Static. "Ned, I'm sorry as hell but I can't locate him along here, maybe he's still on One or maybe he turned off Carmel somewhere. I've lost him . . ."

Quartermain said "Goddamn it!" very softly. Then he depressed the *Send* button on the handset again. "Keep looking, Jim. Go back to One and cruise it. Cruise the side streets off Carmel. I'll put out a surveillance request to the Monterey police and to the State people. Give me a report in five minutes."

Favor acknowledged and signed out, and Quartermain called through to Donovan at the Cypress Bay station and issued his surveillance request. The remainder of the five minutes went by silent and tense, and then Favor came on: negative. Quartermain instructed him to maintain his search until no longer feasible, then he slammed the handset back on the transceiver unit and took us out onto the highway again.

I said, "Winestock won't get far, if running is what he's got in mind."

"I know that, but I'm thinking about the bald man. Winestock might have led us right to him."

"There's still time. It'll work out."

"Sure," he said. "Sure it will."

Beach Road came up on the right, and Quartermain slowed and made the turn. We went down the road past the trailer encampment and out onto the bluff face. The wood-sided station wagon of the morning was no longer parked there, and it was otherwise vacant. Quartermain edged up to the guardrail on the left and darkened the car.

I said, "Dancer's car—what I think is Dancer's car—is gone. Maybe he's out somewhere, too, for one reason or another."

"That's all we need."

The wind blowing in from the sea was chill and damp, and the mist out on the horizon shifted and undulated low over the

118

black carpet of the sea. I pulled up the collar on my suit jacket as we crossed to the set of stairs that led downward to the beach shack.

We paused on the landing, looking down. The house was shrouded in darkness. You could see the breakers spitting foam and spray as they soared up and over the series of bird-limed boulders on either side of the structure, further down; and you could hear the dull throb of the sea's heart, and the sandy whisper of the wind, and the faint sighing of the old, sea-wormed boarding.

"It looks deserted, all right," Quartermain said.

"Do we go through the motions here, too?"

"We might as well. You never know."

We started down the sand-coated steps, moving carefully; the stairs were too narrow for more than one person at a time, and I led the way. We were a third of the way down, and I had my head up looking at the shack, when a flash of flickering red-orange illuminated the night sky immediately to the rear of it.

I stopped, thinking: What the hell was that? The flaring reddish brightness diminished into a dull glow, and all at once I thought: Fire, oh Jesus, *fire!*

I lunged forward, yelling it over my shoulder to Quartermain, running now and hanging onto the railing to keep from losing my balance on the sand-slick boards. I could hear Quartermain cursing steadily behind me. I jumped the last five steps, stumbling, bringing myself upright—and the running figure materialized to the left rear of the shack, racing diagonally toward the rock jetty on that side.

Quartermain saw him at the same time, and he shouted "Stop! Halt there! Police officer!" as we pounded around the side of the shack and down the incline toward the ocean. The running figure slowed momentarily, looking back over his shoulder, and for that instant he was clearly outlined against the pale, starlit black of the sky. Short, wedge-shaped, thick-chested. And even at that distance, because he wore no head covering of any kind, I could see the faint gleam of his bare crown.

The balding guy—the goddamn balding guy.

He swung his head frontally again and kept on running, almost to the rocks down there. Quartermain began to shout again, more in rage than with any thought of the words having an effect. I stayed abreast of him several more steps, and then I thought about the shack and looked back and the glow had brightened somewhat, wavering and flickering. I made one of those instantaneous decisions you have to make in moments of crisis, and shouted to Quartermain, "I'm going to the house!"

He ran on in his loose, shambling way—and the guy was at the rock jetty now, clambering up over the eroded boulders. I took myself out of it, turning, and ran to the sun porch at the rear of the shack, caught the log railing and lifted myself up and over. The drapes were still open across the plate-glass rear wall, and I could see the smoke billowing in there and the flames in a shimmering cherry-yellow pyre; Dancer's bookshelves, the entire left-hand wall, were ablaze.

I went to the porch door, caught the knob and hit the wood paneling with my shoulder at the same time. It banged inward and I was inside, with my right arm up to protect my face. The searing heat of the flames washed over me, and the smoke burned like acid in my lungs, gagging me, taking away my breath. My eyes began to sting and water, and I slitted them, blinking rapidly, looking around the room. Nobody on the floor, nobody on the smoldering furniture—no sign of Dancer. A gasoline can lying to one side, flaming, told me all I needed to know about the origin of the fire.

I ran across to the center hall, coughing violently now, and looked into the kitchen. Empty. I threw open the doors to the bedroom and bathroom, and there was no one in either of them; the place was unoccupied—and that told me something, too. I looked back into the front room, but the fire had begun to spread rapidly and the smoke and flames formed an impenetrable barrier; the roar of the inferno was deafening.

Turning, I stumbled to the front door. It was key-locked, and the key was gone. I hit the panel a couple of times with my shoulder, but it failed to give. Panic formed in the pit of my stomach, clawing. I kicked it down and plunged through the bedroom door, with the smoke and the heat coming hungrily in after me, and got to the window and tugged at the sash and felt it yield and threw it all the way up. My fingers fumbled at the catch-lock on the shutters, snapped it free, and I shoved them apart and dragged myself over the sill and fell onto the sandy ground outside. Half crawling, half running, I got away from there and around onto the slope that fell away to the murmuring surf.

I knelt with my head hanging down, coughing and retching and sucking cold salt air fishlike through my open mouth. When I could breathe again, when some of the burning pain subsided in my lungs, I got my head up and saw Quartermain running toward me from the direction of the near rock jetty. He was alone, and I did not need to ask to know that he'd come up empty; but at least he appeared to be unhurt.

He got to me and took my arm and helped me up. "Are you all right? Christ!"

"I think . . . so."

"Dancer?"

"Not in there. It's empty."

"Bastard got away. He went over the boulders and up a steep bluff down the way. I heard a car engine, and by the time I got up there he was gone. If I'd worn my goddamn gun, I might have had him—son of a bitch, anyway!"

Panting, I pivoted and looked at the shack. Smoke rolled up into the misty sky in thick clouds, and you could see the flames licking with curled orange tongues through the shingled roof. As

I watched, the rear glass wall shattered from the intense heat, bursting smoke and glistening shards and more tongues of fire outward. There was nothing we could do; the place was a damned tinderbox.

Quartermain's face looked hellish in the dancing light. "We'd better get up to the car before a spark catches the stairs," he said savagely, and we ran in a wide sweep toward the bluff wall and along it to the stairs. I could feel the heat again and taste the smoke as we scrambled up. I stopped on the landing, hanging onto the railing and looking down at the flaming shack; Quartermain continued on to the car, and a moment later I could hear him shouting into the transceiver's handset.

I stayed where I was, letting the cool sea wind act as a balm on the heat-reddened surface of my face. Breathing was still a problem, but I thought that it would be all right after a while. A minute or two slid away, and I began to think about the blazing bookshelves and the can of gasoline and the emptiness of the shack, and what meaning those facts had. I turned and went over to the car.

Quartermain was leaning wearily against the roof, the handset still in his fingers and the door open; his iron-colored hair was disarrayed, jutting up and out at angles from his scalp. I said, "I think I know why the fire was set, Ned."

He moved his head in a quadrant and put his eyes on mine; they contained a thinly controlled fury. "Say it."

"There was a can of gasoline in there; the bald guy doused it over Dancer's bookshelves and touched them off. Dancer wasn't home, but the guy still set the fire—and because there were better places to soak up the gasoline, he had to have picked the bookshelves for a specific reason."

Quartermain saw it immediately. "To destroy any copies of *The Dead and the Dying* Dancer might have had."

"Yeah."

"But why?"

"He doesn't want us to read that book," I said. "There's something in it, something in the writing itself. It has to be that way. What the something is we'll know when we read the book —or he figures we will."

"How does he know we haven't already read it?"

"Maybe by my actions, and yours—the police. Maybe we'd be doing things differently if we knew why the book was important."

Quartermain straightened, and his canted eyelids came down. "All right, then," he said. "We've got to read the book."

"The sooner the better."

"Where did you say Paige's copy was—the one I gave you?"

"My unit at the Beachwood, on the nightstand."

"Then we'd better get it."

"Fast," I said. "Before something happens to that one, too."

He called through to Donovan again; Favor had returned to the Cypress Bay station—there was still no report on Winestock—and Quartermain told him to get over to the Beachwood and into my cottage for the book. Favor said he was on his way.

Leaning inside, Quartermain replaced the handset. Then we went over to the stairs again, and the shack was nothing more than a black-and-orange shell now; the roof had collapsed, and sparks drifted and flared in a brilliantine, joyless fireworks display. By the time the county fire equipment got there, not much would be left, not much at all.

Quartermain said tightly, "If that bastard came here to get rid of copies of *The Dead and the Dying*, why wouldn't he be thinking about Dancer too? Dancer *wrote* the damned book."

"He might have been. Maybe, if Dancer had been here, he was supposed to go up along with the shack." I paused grimly. "Or it could be he already got to Dancer, somewhere else."

"I don't want to think about that possibility," Quartermain

said. And then, with sharp frustration: "Goddamn it, I don't understand what's going on. I don't understand any of this. Who in God's name is that guy?"

"Yeah," I said, "who?"

I could hear ululating sirens in the distance, coming down from the north and then coming west from Highway 1 along Beach Road, very loud now. Pretty soon a couple of bright-red county pump engines and a fire marshal's car and a State Highway Patrol unit came out to fill the bluff face with darting light and screaming noise. I retreated to Quartermain's car, and he went over to talk to the marshal. Black-uniformed, white-helmeted men came off the trucks and went to work with hoses and pumping units, and after a time they began playing streams of pressurized water down onto the burning shack.

I sat on the front seat of the car, with the door open and my feet on the ground. My chest was band-tight, but I could breathe all right now if I took the air in short, shallow inhalations. Pain rushed through my temples and behind my eyes, dull and heavy, and I felt vaguely nauseated.

Quartermain came over finally, and I stood up. He said, "You look rough. How do you feel?"

"I'll make it."

"I can radio for a doctor."

"I don't need one."

"All right."

We watched the firemen working with their hoses. The smoke drifting to the south and commingling with the incoming mist formed a curtain of black-flecked grayness over the stars. With the noise created by the men and the pump engines, and local residents attracted by the arrival of the fire units, I could no longer hear the sound of the surf. It would have been no comfort anyway.

The transceiver set began to make crackling noises. Quartermain slid in under the wheel, motioning me around to the

124

other side, and closed the door. When I got in on the passenger side, and shut that door, I could hear Favor's voice saying, ". . . here at the Beachwood now, Ned. Orchard gave me a key to the cabin, but once I got inside I could see that something was wrong. The rear glass door was open, and when I checked I found jimmy marks on the lock."

Oh, I thought. Oh, oh, oh.

Quartermain hit the *Send* switch. "What about the book?"

"It's gone," Favor said.

Fourteen

We left the bluff face and Beach Road immediately, and drove to the Beachwood in Cypress Bay. The book was the only thing missing, nothing else had been touched, and it seemed obvious the balding man—it had to have been him, all right—had used the cover of darkness to come over the hedge or gate into the cottage's private rear garden. Favor had dusted the sliding door and the nightstand with his kit, but there were no prints; the guy had wiped everything clean. Quartermain told him to get in touch with a local artist named Vance, who did portrait work for them from time to time, and to have him waiting at the station to work up a drawing; then we drove over to Bonificacio Drive to talk to Beverly Winestock.

Neither of us expected any help from her—she was too fiercely loyal to her brother for one thing; and I had my doubts he would have told her where he was going tonight—but Quartermain had to talk to her anyway. At the moment, there was no one else he *could* talk to.

Beverly answered the door fully dressed—and still cool, still distant. But her eyes contained a touch of fear, and there were strain lines etched at the corners of her mouth. She was worried, apprehensive, and trying desperately not to show it. She noticed the condition of my face and clothing immediately, and what little color existed in her cheeks drained away. Had something happened, was Brad—?

Quartermain told her, succinctly, about the fire-gutting of Dancer's cabin, and the reason for it, and the theft of Paige's copy of *The Dead and the Dying* from my motel cottage. None of it seemed to have much effect on her; it was, I thought, as if she knew her brother was involved in all of this, but not the *why* or the *how* of his involvement. Quartermain began to question her, but she gave him nothing in response. No, she didn't know where her brother had gone tonight; no, she knew of no connection between Brad and a man answering the description of the balding guy; no, she had no idea why Dancer's book was so important, she had never read it and she knew nothing about it. She wanted to know what it was we suspected Brad of, and Quartermain told her only that he seemed to have information which would assist the investigation into the death of Walter Paige and the location of the balding man. Well, she said, she didn't know anything about Paige's death and she was certain Brad didn't either, we were misguided if we thought he did. There was sincerity in her voice, but you could tell she was holding an intangible something back and would keep on holding it back as long as necessary to protect her brother.

Quartermain gave it up, finally; we left her looking far more worried than she had already been, and drove to City Hall. The only thing cheering or positive waiting for us there was the news that Judith Paige had met her flight out of Monterey on time, had arrived safely at San Francisco International, and had been transported home to Glen Park by someone on the Airport Detail. Donovan had obtained the license number of Russell Dancer's car from Sacramento, and broadcast that as well as the description of Dancer that I had supplied, but there was no word as yet on man or vehicle. Winestock, too, was still among the missing. Quartermain had changed the surveillance request on him to another pick-up order, and had also posted a man at the Winestock house to bring him in if he happened to show up there undetected.

The balding guy's description had also been broadcast to all local and state units, but the type of car he was driving was still unknown and there was not much chance of his being picked up until a picture of him could be circulated. Favor was waiting with the artist, Vance—a short, fat man with bright eyes—to take care of that.

The four of us went to Quartermain's office, and I left them there to use his private bathroom and its stock of first-aid supplies. I stripped down to my underwear and washed off in cool water and put salve on a still-reddened area across my left cheekbone. There was not much I could do about the charred odor which permeated my clothing, but I brushed coat and trousers as best I could and washed a streak of dirt out of the front of my shirt. Then I dressed again and ate half a dozen aspirin for my headache and combed my hair and went in to join the others.

We spent the next forty minutes working with Vance on a drawing of the balding guy. Quartermain had only glimpsed him briefly at Dancer's, but I had seen him fairly close up in the park the day before and I was able to supply enough details—and Vance was skillful enough—so that we came up with what I thought was a pretty good likeness. Once I was satisfied Vance could not improve his sketch, Quartermain told the artist to make printed copies for local distribution and to get the likeness on the wire to Sacramento for possible criminal identification. Vance nodded and left immediately.

I sank wearily into the free armchair next to Favor, and Quartermain said, "You look pretty well frayed at the edges. Maybe you'd better go back to the Beachwood and try to get some sleep."

I felt wrung out, but still uneasily keyed up and wide awake;

128

the last thing I seemed to want was bed and rest. I said, "If it's all the same, I'll sit it out with you."

"No objections," he said. "But it may be a long night."

"It's been a long one already. I can stand it, I think."

He called out for coffee and sandwiches, and the stuff arrived in a couple of minutes; they apparently had some kind of kitchen facility in the building. I tried one of the sandwiches without much interest, and then found I was hungrier than I expected. I put away three of them and two cups of coffee.

There had not been much talking done about things since Beach Road, although Quartermain had apparently briefed Favor while I was in the bathroom, and we were ripe for it now. Quartermain said to us, "Well, all right, what have we got altogether? We've got a dead man named Walter Paige; an unidentified woman who slept with Paige just before he was killed; a bald man who also saw Paige shortly before he was killed, who was seen with Brad Winestock, who set fire to Russell Dancer's home, who broke into the Beachwood, and who damned well wants to keep anyone from reading a twenty-year-old paperback mystery novel. We've got the book itself—or rather, we don't have it and we don't know why it's important; we don't have Winestock, either, *or* Dancer. And then there's Paige trying to rent a vacant store in Cypress Bay for some unknown reason; and two local families acting peculiar, if nothing else, about their relationship with the dead man; and a missing writer who had some kind of trouble with the dead man six years ago; and Winestock's sister covering up in some way for her brother. Add it all together and what does it make? Nothing but a goddamn pot of confusion. So how do we make sense out of it? What's the common denominator? The book?"

"That's the way it looks for now," I said. "It's at least a major part of the key, although it might not necessarily explain Paige's woman's part, or Paige's death for that matter."

"You don't think the bald guy killed Paige?"

"It's not a certainty, especially now that he's gone to so much trouble to suppress copies of Dancer's book. If he killed Paige, why didn't he take the book out of Paige's bag on Saturday? It was sitting there in plain sight."

"He might have been too intent on murder to notice it," Favor said. "Or, if his motive had nothing directly to do with the book itself, he might not have thought about it until later on."

"The woman could even be his motive," Quartermain said, "assuming the possibility that she was his property and Paige was cutting him out. Sure, the two of them were buddy-buddy in the park, but the bald man could have gone to the Beachwood later for some reason, caught Paige and the woman together, lost his head, and killed Paige in a jealous fury."

"Another possibility could be that the woman is entirely innocent of anything except sleeping with Paige. His death could have been the result of a falling out with the bald man, something that happened between them after the woman left Paige's cottage—and, as you say, Ned, despite their apparent friendliness in the park. Something connected with the book, maybe."

Quartermain nodded thoughtfully. "That book," he said, and looked at me. "Did you happen to read any of it this morning?"

"The jacket blurb and the first five pages of text," I answered. "That's all."

"Enough so you can tell us what the thing's about?"

"Not really. As far as I know, this guy comes home from the Korean War and gets mixed up with a bunch of hoods and some hard-assed dames; one of the women, I gathered, talks him into some sort of double-cross and the two of them go on the run with two hundred grand."

"There's not much in that, is there?"

"Not much."

130

"Well, what about the characters? Recognizable as anybody from around here—any of the involved parties? That could be what this is all about; Dancer could have written about some of our local people, thinly disguised, and opened up some closets in the bargain . . ."

"I don't think so," I said. "The book is almost twenty years old, remember—and Paige, for example, was in his early thirties and the others are all pretty much in that same general age bracket. And the novel's protagonist and the first of the women seemed standard types—no special characteristics."

Quartermain finger-combed his hair tiredly. "All right, the hell with it for now. Let's look at some other things. For instance, how the guy knew you had a copy of the book at the Beachwood."

"He had to have been tipped off about it," I said. "There's no other way he could have known. I took it from here directly to the motel this morning, and I doubt if I was being watched at the time."

"Who knew you had it?"

"I mentioned it to everyone I talked with, but as far as I can remember, the only one I told that it was in my possession was Beverly Winestock."

"I thought as much. She told her brother, and Winestock told the bald guy—probably by telephone, either just before or just after we paid our first visit to the Winestock house. Once he knew you had the book and that questions were being asked about it, he figured it was only a matter of time before it was read, so he went after Paige's copy and any that Dancer might have had."

"Which means he knew beforehand that Dancer lived in this area," I said. "Winestock might have told him, or Paige, or he could know Dancer personally even though Dancer claims not to know him."

"Where do you think Winestock went tonight? The bald guy was at the Beachwood and down doing the job on Dancer's place."

"Maybe to wait for him to come back," Favor said. "Monterey, since that's where I lost Winestock, or somewhere north or east of here—not Cypress Bay, though."

I shifted in my chair. "There's a pattern to this thing somewhere, a kind of wheel with Paige and that book and the bald man as the hub, and Winestock and Beverly Winestock and the Lomaxes and the Tarrants—some of them, at least—as the spokes. It's nebulous as hell, but it's there. If we only had the book . . ."

"Or Dancer," Quartermain said. "Listen, you collect pulp magazines. How easy would it be to dig up another copy of *The Dead and the Dying*, assuming Dancer can't or won't help us? How fast could it be done?"

"An obscure paperback title like that—it might take considerable time and effort. I know a couple of book dealers in San Francisco that specialize in magazines and used paperbacks. If they don't have it in stock—and chances are they wouldn't—they could put a line out to other dealers or to collectors of crime fiction who might have it or know where it could be gotten. All of which would take time, as I said. And I've got the feeling time is an important factor; the bald guy has got to know we'll dig up a copy of the book eventually, and yet he still went to a hell of a lot of trouble tonight to get rid of immediately available copies."

"I thought of that, too, and it only complicates things that much more. How the hell could a time element enter into it?"

"No ideas," I said, "and no guesses."

"Ditto," Favor said.

Quartermain slumped back in his chair; the purplish bags under his deep-set and slant-lidded eyes made him look like a kind of Oriental hound. "If Dancer doesn't turn up by morning, and with the right answers, you can call those book dealers of yours and get them to work," he said to me. "There's a place in Monterey, I think, that handles used paperback books and we'll try them too. Other than that, there's nothing we can do about the book. No goddamn thing at all."

None of us seemed to feel much like talking after that, and a brooding, waiting silence formed thickly in there. I sat and stared at nothing and wanted a cigarette and kept on resisting the urge. A sunburst clock on one wall ticked away the minutes loudly and monotonously, and I saw that we were now two hours into a new day—into a new month, too, for that matter, since Sunday had been the last day of April. Monday. Blue Monday—or black Monday, take your choice. Some choice.

More time passed, and nothing happened. Three A.M. Four A.M. Quartermain sat tipped back in his chair, his eyes closed, and Favor began to snore gently in the armchair beside mine. The warm room and the inactivity and the lack of sleep and the physical enervation began to exact their toll on me as well; you can resist for only so long. I was down in that vague, heavy, slow-motion world between sleep and wakefulness, drifting toward oblivion, when Quartermain's telephone bell went off.

I came up out of my chair convulsively, pawing at my eyes and looking blankly around, my heart plunging in my chest and my head banging malignantly. When the misty remnants of sleep dissolved, I saw Quartermain swiveling around to drag up the phone receiver and Favor sitting forward in his chair, smoothing his mustache in an unconscious gesture that made him look more than ever like a silent-movie comedian. I sat down again and dry-washed my face, listening, but Quartermain said "Yeah" and "Christ!" and "Right away" and that was all.

I looked up at him as he replaced the handset. His mouth was pinched tight at the corners and his nostrils were flared and his eyes were hot, bright chunks of blue, like dry ice smoldering.

Favor said, "What is it, Ned?"

133

"That was the State Highway Patrol. They've just located Winestock's Studebaker."

"Where?"

"Spanish Bay, just south of Pacific Grove."

"What about Winestock?"

"He's in it," Quartermain said. "Shot twice in the chest and stone-cold dead."

Fifteen

Dawn had begun to streak the eastern sky by the time we got out to Spanish Bay, on the northwestern shore of the Monterey Peninsula. In the cold gray light the panoramic landscape of cypress and windswept, bone-white sand dunes had a hushed and primitive look, like a tiny portion of nature that had long ago been suspended in time. The sea beyond provided the only motion; it was a rippling gray-green, the combers high and capped with garlands of white froth as they crested and rolled downward in long, graceful sweeps to the beach.

Just after we began to skirt the boundary of the Asilomar Beach State Park, the small cluster of cars appeared among all that quiet beauty like a giant's thoughtlessly discarded litter. They were drawn close together near a low fan of cypress, two-thirds of the way along an unpaved lane that led toward the symmetrically spaced dunes and the splendor of the Pacific. Favor cut off the siren we had used to make time from Cypress Bay and took us down the lane. As we approached the cluster, I could distinguish five vehicles: a State Highway Patrol unit, an unmarked sedan, a Pacific Grove Police Department tow truck, a county ambulance, and Brad Winestock's faded-blue Studebaker. Both doors on the driver's side of the Studebaker were standing open, and several men were grouped in a tight knot nearby, talking among themselves and watching our arrival.

Favor pulled up behind the sedan, and the three of us got out into a wind that was chill and yet tinged with the spring warmth that would come with the rising sun. Four of the seven men on the scene were official: a local patrol investigator named Daviault, two patrol officers in uniform, and an assistant county coroner. The other three were a pair of ambulance attendants and the driver of the wrecker, who would tow Winestock's car into Pacific Grove or Monterey for the crime-lab technicians. Quartermain introduced me briefly to Daviault, and he accepted my presence without question.

He led us to the Studebaker, and we looked inside. Winestock was in the back, sprawled across the seat face up; his eyes were protuberant, with much of the whites showing—as if the impact of the bullets or the intensity of his dying had been enough to half pop them from their sockets. There was coagulated blood on the front of his windbreaker, and some on the seat beneath him—but altogether, very little. That, and the fact that both wounds were visibly centered on the upper part of his chest, said that he had died swiftly.

I turned away, dry-mouthed, and Quartermain asked the two uniformed patrolmen, "Were you the ones who found him?"

"Yes, sir," one of them said. "We were cruising Sunset Drive and we spotted the car down here; at first we thought it might be kids parked for the night, and we came down to chase them off. When we got close enough, we saw that it was the Studebaker on our pickup sheet. We found him inside there, just the way you see him."

"How long ago was that?"

"A little more than an hour."

"Did you check the hood then for engine heat?"

"Yes, sir. It was cold."

"Do you patrol this area regularly?"

"Once or twice a night."

"Had you been along here earlier?"

"No, sir. This was our first swing through."

Quartermain said to Daviault, "What about the gun?"

"No sign of it."

"Anything in the car?"

"Nothing unusual. Same for the trunk."

"Outside it?"

"No," Daviault said. "The road surface won't sustain tire impressions, as you can see."

"No leads at all then."

"Nothing we've been able to turn up so far."

Quartermain looked at the assistant coroner. "Can you make a preliminary guess as to how long he's been dead?"

"A rough guess, if that's what you want."

"I'll take it for now."

"From the temperature and condition of the body, I'd say no more than six hours, no less than three."

"Do you think he was killed in the car or somewhere else?"

"Difficult to tell. There are no exit wounds, so he's still carrying the two bullets inside him; no powder burns, so he was apparently shot at a distance. That might be significant, considering the close confines of the car. Then again, there's a little blood on the seat and he didn't bleed much after he was shot; death was likely instantaneous, or very close to it."

I moved away from the group and stood looking out to sea; I had heard all there was to hear for now, even though they were still talking it through. Some distance offshore, on a group of tiny rock islands, the dark shapes of cormorants and loons moved and fluttered and sat in sentinel-like motionlessness— and nearby a sleek black or brown sea lion came up out of the water like an iridescent phantom. The peach color of dawn had spread and modulated into soft gold, consuming the gray, and it would not be long before sunrise. It was going to be another fine spring day.

But the climate, as they say, was one of violence.

And pain, I thought. And grief. First Judith Paige—the rape of innocence. And now Beverly Winestock—the bitter fruits of too much family loyalty, and another kick in the groin for a woman who seemed to have been kicked too many times already. How many more were going to suffer? Yeah, how many more? Because it wasn't over yet, and two men were dead already, and Dancer was still missing, and murder and violence invariably beget murder and violence. The tremors beneath the surface of it all had gathered strength now, had become more volatile, had begun to foment further destruction, and you knew with a kind of fatalistic insight just what to expect before it was finally ended . . .

After a time Quartermain came over and said, "We'll be going now; there's nothing more for us here. We've got other things to do."

"All right," I said. I did not ask him what it was we had to do, because the answer was obvious. And it was nothing I cared to put into words just then; the contemplation of it was bitterly cheerless enough.

She opened the door and looked out at the three of us standing there under the bougainvillaeaed arbor—and she knew. It was all there in our faces, unmistakable and irrefutable. Her right hand went out and clawed whitely at the doorjamb, supporting her weight there; her left hand came up to her throat, clutching at the neck of her quilted housecoat in that pathetic little gesture women involuntarily seem to make at such times. Her face was the color of winter slush and her eyes were sick little animals hiding in caves formed by ridges of bone and taut, purplish skin; she was no longer ethereal, no longer hauntingly

138

beautiful, she was an old woman facing the loss of the only real loved one she had in the world. I could not look at her directly any longer. I turned my head away, with emptiness and helplessness heavy inside me; it was the way I had felt facing Judith Paige's grief and the way I would always feel facing any grief at all. And I wondered why I had come, knowing what it would be like—why I had not stayed in the car, why I had not asked them to let me off at City Hall, why I did not get out of it and go the hell home.

Quartermain said gently, "May we come in, Miss Winestock?"

She just stood there, motionless, a chunk of gray stone wrapped in bright-colored quilt. Then her mouth and her throat worked, and she got the words free. She said, "It's Brad, isn't it? He's dead, isn't he?"

Hesitation. You never know what to say, or how to say it. So you pause—and when the pause becomes awkward you say it as Quartermain said it; you say, softly "I'm sorry."

"Oh God," she said. "Oh my God." She was still standing absolutely still: no hysterics, no tears. Just "Oh God, oh my God." And somehow, there in the cold dawn, it was worse than if she had fainted or cried or broken down completely.

There was more heavy silence, and then Quartermain said again, "May we come in, Miss Winestock? It would be better than trying to talk out here."

In mute answer she pushed herself away from the doorjamb and moved stiff-legged down the hall—an animated figurine, brittle and graceless. Favor, Quartermain, and I followed her through the archway and into the parlor. It was dark in there, with the curtains closed, and I touched the wall switch to chase away some of the shadows with suffused light from an overhead fixture. Beverly sat down on one of the chairs, her arms flat on the chair arms; her eyes seemed to be seeing inward instead of outward, glistening like rain puddles under a streetlamp.

We took seats here and there, and the silence grew and became awkward again. Quartermain cleared his throat, and she said "How did it happen?" in a flat, dull voice.

Quartermain answered simply, "He was shot."

The eyes closed, briefly. "Murdered, you mean?"

"Yes."

"Who did it? This bald man you keep asking about?"

"We don't know yet, Miss Winestock."

"But you think it might have been that man."

"There's a good chance of it, yes."

"Where did you find him—Brad?"

"Spanish Bay. In his car."

"I see. And you say he was shot?"

"Yes."

"Did he seem to have had much pain, can you tell me that?"

"No, I don't think he did. No."

"That's good," she said. "That's something anyway."

"Miss Winestock . . ."

"Can I see him? I'd like to see him."

"I'll have a car take you to Monterey. But there are some questions first. Do you feel up to answering a few questions?"

"Yes. All right."

"Were you telling the truth last night—that you didn't know where your brother had gone?"

"Yes."

"And about the bald man?"

"I don't know who he is. I'd tell you if I had any idea."

"Before he left, did your brother make any phone calls?"

She nodded. "One. Just after you'd gone."

"Did you hear any of the conversation?"

"No. I was out of the room and he spoke too softly."

"Then you don't know who he called, or what number?"

"No."

"He said nothing to you before he went out?"

"I asked him where he was going, I begged him to stay home. He wouldn't talk to me."

"Did he talk to you when he came home yesterday afternoon?"

"No. He was very nervous—afraid. He told me to leave him alone and then he started drinking, just sitting in here drinking by himself."

"Was he mixed up in the killing of Walter Paige?"

"I . . . I'm not sure. He didn't kill Walt, he wasn't capable of killing anyone. And he was home on Saturday; he told you that. I overheard part of your conversation with him."

"Do you think he knew who did kill Paige?"

"He might have. He was very afraid."

"He was involved in something, wasn't he? Something to do with Paige."

"Yes. Yes."

"What?"

"I don't know."

"You're holding something back," he said. "You've been holding something back all along. I think you'd better tell what it is, Miss Winestock."

She exhaled tremulously, and there were deep, shadowed hollows in her cheeks and her eyes seemed ringed in black in the room's pale light; she was a century old, sitting there, and aging more rapidly with each passing minute. "There's no point in not telling you now. It's too late now, isn't it?" She sighed again. "Brad let himself get talked into some kind of scheme of Walt Paige's; he was like a little boy, you could talk him into anything once you got him to listen to you. Walt called him on the phone several weeks ago—out of the blue, after six years—and Brad met him somewhere later on. I think he saw him on other occasions after that."

"Here in Cypress Bay?"

"Yes, as far as I know."

"Then you knew Paige had come back to the area, that he had been here off and on for several weeks."

"I suspected it."

"But you never saw Paige yourself?"

"No."

"Did you ask your brother what Paige wanted, why he had called after all those years?"

"Yes. Brad wouldn't tell me. But he talked about going away, about having enough money to buy a boat down in Florida and go island-hopping. That was always his dream, to have a boat of his own in the Florida Keys." She laughed emptily. "I think he got that idea from reading Hemingway."

"That's all he would tell you?"

"Yes. He seemed constantly excited, constantly on edge. It worried me. Brad was never . . . well, never too bright in addition to being easily swayed. I was afraid for him, knowing Walt Paige as I did."

"How do you mean that?"

"The kind of man Walt was—using people, not caring if they got hurt or not. And I always felt there was something a little . . . shady about him. He always had money and he didn't have a job." She seemed to remember that I was in the room, and turned her head slightly to glance at me. "When you told me yesterday that Walt had been in prison for four years, I was even more frightened for Brad. I thought it must have been some kind of crime or something that Walt had talked him into. That's why I didn't say anything about Brad's involvement. I wanted to protect him. I . . . ."

She broke off, closing her eyes, and you could see her blaming herself—hating herself—for not having made some sort of saving decision in her brother's behalf. It was obvious that she had been protecting him for years in her own way, and now she had failed him and he was dead, he was gone forever. It was false logic, and maybe she would realize that later on, when some of the shock wore off; maybe she would fashion another thick layer of skin, as she seemed to have fashioned one on top of the other at past injustices, and go on spitting in life's eye. Maybe she would.

Quartermain was saying, "Did your brother ever mention Russell Dancer's book *The Dead and the Dying?*"

"No," Beverly said. "I'd never even heard of it until yesterday morning. Could it . . . is it really important somehow?"

"It's important, but we don't know how just yet," Quartermain told her. He paused. "Would you mind if we looked around the house—in your brother's room?"

"No, I don't mind," dully. "But there's nothing for you to find. Brad has some books in his room, but they're mostly westerns—and Hemingway. He loved Hemingway, even though I'm sure he never really understood any of the writing. Isn't that strange?"

Quartermain said softly, "Would you show Lieutenant Favor the location of your brother's room?"

"Yes, all right."

Favor helped her up, steadying her with his arm, looking as if he wished to God he was a long, long way from this room and this house; I knew exactly how he felt. They went out through the archway, with Beverly still moving in that brittle, graceless way. Momentarily I could hear them climbing stairs to the second floor.

Quartermain and I began to prowl the parlor, the hall, the kitchen, a dining room, a small sitting room; no copies of Dancer's book—no books at all—and nothing pointing to the balding man or Paige or anyone else connected with the case. We came back into the parlor, and Quartermain said, "Well, what do you think?"

"About her story? I think it's the truth, Ned. She's too grief-stricken to be an effective liar, and to hold anything else back. But she hasn't really given us a great deal except confirmation of her brother's involvement with Paige and of a scheme between the two of them, and we both pretty much suspected that. The bald guy's mixed up in the scheme, too, and so is the book."

"Some kind of crime, she said. That could be what this whole thing is about—a felony of one type or another, with profit as the motive."

"It's beginning to look that way," I agreed. "But it could be just about any kind of felony. The book's back-cover blurb didn't mention any specific crime except murder—and there was nothing in those first five pages I read."

He went over to one of the wall murals and brooded at it until, finally, Favor and Beverly came down the stairs and entered the parlor again. She had put on a dark shirt and blouse and thrown a coat over her shoulders. She had not bothered with her hair—it was still piled loosely on top of her head—and there was still no make-up on her wide mouth; you do not think about personal appearance at a time like this.

Favor came over to where Quartermain and I were standing. "I went through his room and hers, too, after she'd finished dressing. No sign of Dancer's book; two westerns by him, recent issue, but that's all."

"What about an address book—like that?"

Favor shook his head. "If he had anything that might lead to the bald man, he didn't keep it in his room."

"Or anywhere else in the house."

Beverly said, "I'd like to see Brad now, please." The sorrow in her face was stark and piteous. "There's nothing else I can tell you, there's nothing else that I know."

"All right, Miss Winestock."

He used her phone to call Donovan and request a patrol unit to escort her to Peninsula Community Hospital in Monterey, where Winestock's body had been taken. We waited for the car in silence, and it came in ten long minutes, and the four of us went out and down the steps into the bright morning with Beverly trying to hide her trembling hands in the pocket of her coat. At the patrol car Favor said, "It might be a good idea if I went along, Ned," and looked meaningly at Quartermain.

"So it might," he agreed, thinking—as Favor was, as I was too—that it would be easier on her if she had a little more authority at her side to get her in and out of the hospital morgue as quickly as possible. Favor was some cop, and some man; as much as he hated confronting Beverly's grief, he was willing to face it for another hour or two to help ease some of her pain.

He helped her into the patrol car, and it pulled away, and a few moments later Quartermain and I were on our way back to City Hall. The image of Beverly's tragic face was still with me, and I felt a sudden wish that there had been something meaningful for each of us at our first meeting yesterday—some kind of attraction, some kind of magic. But then I thought about Cheryl Rosmond and *her* brother and how it had been for us afterward, and I knew it was far, far better that there had been nothing after all.

Sixteen

We came into City Hall, and Quartermain's office, through the police entrance at the rear. He folded his big, loose body into his chair, picked up the phone, and called out to the front desk. Donovan, it seemed, was plagued by local, San Francisco, and wire-service reporters who had gotten wind of Winestock's murder and the fire-gutting of Dancer's shack. The reporters wanted to know, since Quartermain and I had been on the scene both times, if the events had any connection with the killing on Saturday of Walter Paige. Did the Chief want to come out and give them a statement?

Quartermain was in no mood for reporters. He told Donovan to tell them he had nothing to say at this time, that a statement would be issued when events warranted it; then he asked if there was any word as yet on Russell Dancer or on the balding man. Donovan said that there wasn't. Wearily Quartermain cut off and called the Highway Patrol office in Monterey and talked for a while to Daviault. When he broke that connection, he said to me, "They dug two steel-jacketed thirty-eight slugs out of Winestock, both from the heart region, and they figure death was instantaneous. Probably shot somewhere else and taken to Spanish Bay in the car; the blood on the seat was smeared and

146

there's the absence of powder burns. No prints except Winestock's on the car, inside or out; killer apparently wore gloves. Winestock had nothing helpful in his pockets or his wallet: no address book, no papers with phone numbers or addresses, nothing at all. If he ever had anything, it was removed before the killer got out of there. Another frigging dead end."

I shook my head and glanced up at the sunburst clock; it was seven-forty. "It's still too early to reach the book dealers in San Francisco," I said. "The two I told you about don't open until ten A.M., and I don't know the last names of the owners."

"I'll call the Monterey police, about the bookshop over there; they ought to know the owner, and they can get him out of bed and down to look through his stock. I've got a feeling it won't do much good, but we've got to try it."

He made the call, slapped the receiver down, and looked across at me. "How about some coffee?"

"I don't think so—but you go ahead."

"I guess I don't want any either."

"You know, I can't help thinking now that we could figure out why that damned book is important *without* it and without Dancer—that we know enough facts to be able to make a reasonably accurate guess. But the pieces are so well scattered, and relatively unimportant by themselves, that I can't pick them out and fit them together."

He nodded thoughtfully. "The trouble is, we've been up all night, and we're so close to this whole thing that we maybe can't see the forest for the trees. But we might try going over it again anyway . . ."

We went over it again, and failed to come up with a viable guess, and finally lapsed into a frustrated silence. And more time passed. And nothing happened.

And so you keep on sitting there, willing the phone to ring, the door to open—and the phone remains silent and the door remains closed. You listen to the rhythm of the clock, very loud in

147

the stillness. The chair is uncomfortable, and there is dull pain in your temples and a murkiness to your vision, as if a coat of transparent lacquer had been sprayed over the surface of your eyes. Your throat is dry and gritty, your tongue thick and wrapped in sourness. Your joints feel stiff and atrophied, and your legs ache, and your thoughts are heavy and oddly detached.

You're in fine shape, all right, sitting and waiting and fighting off sleep and not knowing why you're doing it to yourself, why you're there, because you're not getting paid for any of this and the reason you got into it in the first place is sitting home alone in the fine old bitch city San Francisco, where nobody should ever be alone. You should be home, too, you should be out of it, you should be doing something for Judith Paige and for yourself. So why are you here, you wonder, why are you still involved? Because you're a cop and you've always been a cop and you can't let go of the scent once you've got onto it? The old argument—but there's more to it than that, really, you know there is. How about this, then: because it's there—the case, the human folly, the human misery—and you feel you have to surmount it; it's like one in a long string of Everests, only where you're concerned, it isn't mountains but evil. That might be it, that just might be it, because down underneath it all you're a dreamer, a romantic, an optimist masquerading as a bitter realist— you poor tired old bastard you.

I felt as if I were petrifying in the chair and pulled myself up and began to walk around the office. Quartermain was sitting tensely, hands flat on his thighs, his eyes dull and hard. Grayish beard stubble patterned his long cheeks, and his throat, visible where he had long since pulled away his tie, was a V of loose skin hollowed above his collarbone. I thought, looking at him, that he was almost certainly a mirror image of myself—and the thought was somehow a little frightening.

Without thinking about it, I got out a cigarette and put it be-

148

tween my lips and fired it. I had the first drag and then remembered the tender condition of my lungs, but it was not too bad; the smoke burned harshly at first and I coughed a couple of times, and after that it was all right. The taste of it was gray ash, but I smoked it down anyway.

The clock on the wall said it was five past eight.

Quartermain slapped the desk top with the palm of his hand, so abruptly and so sharply that I jumped and wheeled around to look at him again. He stood up. "The hell with this," he said. "This goddamn sitting around is driving me nuts. Let's get out of here, let's go for a ride, let's get something done."

"I'm for that," I said. "Where do we go?"

"Out to Cypress Point."

"The Lomaxes?"

"The Lomaxes," he said. "And they'd damned well better be home when we get there."

They were home.

The entrance gate on Inspiration Way was closed but not locked, and when we got down far enough into the small valley the forest-green Mercedes appeared in front of the terrace wall. Quartermain parked behind it. The front door of the house opened just as we got to it, and Jason Lomax came out and shut the door behind him. He wore an olive-green business suit and a silk tie and alligator-skin shoes, and with his razor-cut hair and barbered mustache, the attire gave him the look of a successful if stuffy advertising or corporation executive. A professional, intelligent smile would have completed the image; but Lomax's mouth was a thin, hard incision, with ridged muscle at the corners, and his eyes held the glitter of synthetic diamonds.

"Morning, Jason," Quartermain said. His tone was deceptively mild, edged with authority, and I knew that even though the Lomaxes were important people in the community of Cypress Bay, too much had happened in the past thirty-six hours for him to use the soft approach; he was not about to stand for any bullshit, no matter what the source or cause.

Lomax said coolly, ignoring me, "Good morning, Chief. Is there something I can do for you?"

"There is. Is your wife here at the moment?"

"Yes, she's here. But I don't think—"

"Shall we go inside? Or do you want to call Robin out here? What we have to talk about concerns her, too."

Lomax stared at him for a long moment, read his haggard face correctly, and said, "All right, then. But I know why you're here, and you're making a very large mistake. I told this man yesterday"—gesturing at me the way you would gesture at a tree stump—"everything my wife and I know about Walter Paige and his death, which amounts to almost nothing at all."

"I hope so, Jason. I hope that's what it amounts to."

Lomax started to say something else, changed his mind, and turned grimly to the door. He opened it and we went inside and into a long, deep living room furnished in eighteenth-century Early American, paneled in maple, floored in *gros point,* and decorated with old-bronze lamps and knick-knacks. Blue drapes were open at a picture window that took up most of the side wall, and beyond you could see the flagstone terrace and, around toward the back, part of a green-tile swimming pool.

Robin Lomax entered by way of a door at the rear of the room. She wore a plain short-sleeved white dress—she was the kind of woman who would wear white whenever possible, because it complimented her tanned skin and because it made her look young and fresh and innocent—and her face was carefully composed, her lips turned in a small, polite smile. But there was faint disapproval and more than a little fear in her eyes as she looked at Quartermain and me, as if in our rumpled, unshaven condition we were derelict intruders come for some dark purpose. The amenities were brief and strained—the polite good mornings, her invitation to sit down, her automatic offer of

150

coffee, which we automatically refused. Then we took a long sofa and the two of them sat in facing chairs and we got to the point of it.

Lomax asked stiffly, "Just what is it you want to ask us, Chief?" His manner continued to negate my presence.

"To begin with, where you were last night."

The question startled them; they had not been prepared for that kind of opener. He said, "Last night?"

"Yes. We came by just after dark, and no one was here."

"Oh, I see. Well, we took Tommy to his grandmother's in Salinas and then we went to dinner and cocktails at Del Monte Lodge."

"You left in something of a hurry, didn't you?"

"Hurry?"

"You neglected to close the front gate, and you forgot to turn on the night-lighting here on the grounds. When you go out for a casual evening, don't you usually attend to those things?"

Robin Lomax moved uncomfortably in her chair and looked at her husband. He said, "We were rather upset. Your private detective's visit accounted for that."

"He's not *my* private detective, Jason."

"He's here with you now. He seemed to have your sanction to come around here yesterday making accusations . . ."

"No one made any accusations, Mr. Lomax," I said evenly.

Quartermain made an angry, impatient gesture. "All right," he said to Lomax, "so you took your son to his grandmother's and then you went out to supper and cocktails at Del Monte."

"Yes," Lomax answered, and nodded.

"Do you normally go out to dinner when you're upset?"

"We had promised Robin's mother that we would bring Tommy to see her, and the drive to Salinas seemed just what both of us needed. We felt much better on the way home, and we decided to stop at the lodge. That's all."

"What time did you leave there?"

"Midnight or shortly after."

"Did you come straight home?"

"Yes, of course. Why are you asking all these questions about last night?"

"Because Brad Winestock was murdered just before or just after midnight—shot to death at Spanish Bay, or somewhere else, and then taken out there in his car."

Robin Lomax made a small, shocked sound and reached out in a blind sort of way to pluck at her husband's arm again. He just sat there, staring at us. "Who did it? Who would want to kill a poor nothing like Brad Winestock?"

"Very possibly the same person who killed Walter Paige."

"And we're under suspicion for both crimes, is that it?"

"I didn't say you were under suspicion, did I, Jason?"

"Well, you're acting as if we are, coming here with your questions and your intimations. We're respectable people, for God's sake, and I resent your trying to involve us in sordidness and murder."

"I'm *not* trying to involve you, I'm trying to do my job the best way I know how. Now, the two of you knew Paige six years ago and you knew Brad Winestock; you reacted violently when confronted by Paige's name yesterday, and you seemed hardly willing to answer questions pertaining to Paige and your relationship with him. Those are the simple facts, and I'm here to find out the reasons for them. As long as you cooperate, and as long as you have nothing to hide, I'll apologize for my intrusion and for any inconvenience and you won't be bothered again. I don't see the need for indignation in any of that—unless you *do* have something to hide."

"We have nothing to hide," Lomax said.

"Fine. Now suppose you tell me about Walter Paige, and why you were so upset at the mention of his name yesterday."

Lomax and his wife exchanged glances—they were good at exchanging glances—and again I could see nothing of any significance pass between them. He said, "Very well. I'll tell you why Walter Paige was and still is a filthy name around here, and I'll tell you why both my wife and I are glad he's dead even though we had absolutely nothing to do with his death."

He paused, and took a long breath, and went on, "Paige thought he was irresistible, and that every woman in the world ought to fall fawning at his feet. Well, Robin didn't fall and that hurt his ego. So he got her somewhat . . . intoxicated one night, after she'd had a minor argument with me—we were going together at the time, you see—and he tried to attack her. She fought him off and managed to get away from him, but it was a very messy business, as you can well imagine. Naturally, when she told me, I wanted to attend to Paige personally, but we both saw the folly of that. We simply put the matter out of our minds as best we could, and shortly afterward Paige left Cypress Bay. We thought he had gone for good. When we heard he was back"—looking at me now, finally acknowledging my presence —"and this was before you told us of his death, you may remember, we were both angry and upset."

"And that's all there is to it?" Quartermain asked.

"Absolutely all."

The hell it is, I thought. I said, "You seemed almost as unnerved by the fact that I was a private detective as you were by my mention of Paige's name. Why, Mr. Lomax?"

His eyes flared with a kind of unreasonable hatred for me, and then he blinked and it was gone. Mrs. Lomax worked on her lower lip with her sharp white teeth; the fear was still in her eyes and she seemed to be having difficulty maintaining her composure.

Quartermain said, "Answer his question, Jason."

"We're not at all used to being visited by private detectives, right out of nowhere on a Sunday afternoon." Lomax's voice was brittle again. "Naturally we were surprised and a little taken aback. Private detectives, if you can believe television and films, are hardly the type of people one likes to be confronted with unexpectedly."

God, what a supercilious bastard! What he knew about private detectives you could put in a goddamn thimble; what he knew about a lot of things—including natural human emotions and compassions—you could put in a goddamn thimble. I looked at Quartermain, but I could not tell from his expression what he thought of Lomax's rehearsed-sounding and pompous answers.

He said, "You were both here between four and six o'clock Saturday afternoon, is that right?"

"Yes," she said, "that's right."

"Playing tennis," Lomax added.

"And you hadn't seen or heard from Walter Paige in six years?"

"Yes. Or rather, no."

"And you've never heard of a book of Russell Dancer's called *The Dead and the Dying*."

"Certainly not."

"And you don't know a fortyish, kind of bald man who was apparently a friend of Paige's and of Winestock's."

"No."

"Do you have anything more to tell me, about anything at all we've discussed just now or which might have any bearing on either or both murders?"

Lomax moistened his lips. "No," he said, "we have nothing more to tell you, Chief."

"Then I'll take you at your word," Quartermain said, "and hope for your sakes that I don't have to come back again with more questions." He stood up and I stood up with him. "Thanks for your time, Jason, and yours, Robin."

Lomax started to get up, but Quartermain told him we could find our own way out and muttered a good morning. I followed him across to the door and out and through the facing garden to his car. Once inside, he said, "They're holding something back, too, the stubborn goddamn fools. Jesus Christ, I can't get a straight story out of anybody!"

I did not say anything; I had nothing to offer on the subject of the Lomaxes. Their involvement, whatever it was, was too nebulous at this point to make conjecture worthwhile. Quartermain had taken his questioning as far as he could without getting tough, and you don't get tough with people like the Lomaxes unless you've got something definite to back you up. As it was, there would no doubt be repercussions from the City Fathers once Lomax, being the kind of man he was, got through screaming about police harassment. It took a lot of guts, I thought, for Quartermain to handle things as he had—to allow me to keep my unofficial hand in. He's a good cop, a hell of a good cop, and he deserves better than he's getting. He deserves a break. And soon, damned soon.

As if reading my thoughts, he said as he started the car, "God, I wish things would open up for us before long, before anything else happens. I wish we could get a break, just one little break."

And we got one.

Just like that, just as if all you had to do was ask for it in the right kind of thoughts and words.

Donovan called on the transceiver while we were driving back to City Hall. He had just had a report from the county sheriff's unit which Quartermain had earlier asked be posted on Beach Road: they were on their way into Cypress Bay, and they were bringing with them—badly hungover but otherwise alive and well—the driver of an old wood-sided station wagon that had turned up at nine-ten.

The driver's—and the break's—name was Russell Dancer.

Seventeen

Dancer was badly hungover, all right—his hands trembled vaguely and his eyes were bas-reliefed with blood-red veins and the skin of his face was loose and alternately splotched red and gray—but the intake of too much alcohol was only part of the reason for his sick condition. He had seen what was left of his beach shack, his home, his possessions, perhaps the last of his dreams; and the sight seemed to have unleashed a toxic, destructive combination of bitterness and frustration and self-pity inside him, joining with the hangover symptoms to give him a zombielike appearance as he came slowly, stiffly, through the door of Quartermain's office. He may have been guilty of or responsible for or involved in some of the things that had happened in Cypress Bay this past weekend, or six years ago, but I felt immediate compassion for him just the same; he was still a lonely man, and even though it was nothing I could have put into the right kind of words, I could understand something of the depth of his loss and of his feeling.

He looked at me first, and his mouth twisted into a ghost of his wry smile. "I thought you were getting out and going back to San Francisco," he said. His voice was hollow and burned out, the words thickened by the dry rolling movement of his tongue.

"But here you are, looking like you've been up all night in the bargain."

"I *have* been up all night," I said. "Some things happened to change my mind about leaving and about becoming involved."

"So you're no different than the standard fictional private dick, after all. Or maybe you are. I can't decide which."

Quartermain said, "Sit down, Dancer. You look like you'd better have some coffee."

"Unless you've got a little hair of the dog."

"Just coffee. Black?"

"God, yes."

Quartermain motioned to the two county patrol cops who had escorted Dancer from Beach Road, and the Cypress Bay uniformed officer who had come in with them through the police entrance at the building's rear. They turned and went out into the anteroom, where the office secretary was back on duty and banging away on his typewriter, and Quartermain and I followed. He shut the door, dismissed the uniform, told the secretary to get a pot of hot black coffee, and then looked at the two county cops.

"Dancer tell you where he's been all night?" he asked.

"Yes, sir, on the way in," one of them said. "He claims to have been shacked up with an old girl friend and a bottle, and that his car was parked in her garage all night."

"Where?"

"Jamesburg."

"Would he tell you the girl friend's name?"

"Yes, sir. It's Verna Nunnally."

The other cop said, "A widow—or so he claimed."

"What about an address?" Quartermain asked.

"That too: Los Piños Drive. We radioed over to Jamesburg for a check, and as soon as it's made they'll contact you direct."

"Good, thanks. Did Dancer have anything else to say?"

"He seemed pretty shaken up by what happened to his

place," the first cop said. "I don't blame him much; it's a hell of a thing to have to come home to."

"He wanted to know how it happened," the second cop said. "We didn't tell him anything; we didn't know how you wanted it handled."

Quartermain nodded. "That's it?"

"Yes, sir, that's about it."

He thanked them again and told them they could go. The secretary came in with the coffee as they were leaving, and I took the pot from him and we went into the inner office again. Dancer was sitting in one of the armchairs, holding his head in both hands. He brought the hands down as Quartermain went around the desk and I went up to it and poured him some coffee.

"Angel of mercy," he said dully, and took the cup I handed him. He held it between both palms and stared into it for a time, and then raised it shakily to his lips and drank a little. I sat down and looked at him; Quartermain had a hip cocked against the rear edge of the desk, leaning forward.

He said, "We've been trying to find you ever since ten o'clock last night. I understand you were in Jamesburg."

"Yeah. Celebrating the completion of my latest western epic with a piece of tail and some bonded bourbon. Dancer fiddling while his Rome burns. What a lousy fucking thing."

"What time did you leave your place last night?"

"Eight or a little before, I think. I finished the last page around seven and had a shower and changed my clothes; then I took the manuscript and went up to the Mount Royal Bar." The bitter, ghostly smile again. "That's something, at least—the manuscript. I was going to mail it today, so I took it with me. I've still got that much anyway. A whole hell of a lot, all right."

I said, "You didn't have any personal property insurance?"

"Oh sure, I've got personal property insurance; I'm not stupid enough to live in a place like that without it. But there are some things you can't replace with insurance money."

"Yeah," I said, and I thought I knew what some of those things were.

Quartermain asked, "How long were you at the Mount Royal last night?"

"Long enough to have a couple of drinks and decide I was horny and to call Verna over in Jamesburg. That's Verna Nunnally, a friend of my ex-wife's. I take a perverse pleasure in banging friends of my ex-wife's. She was home and I drove over there with a bottle and spent the night and drove back this morning." He got the coffee cup to his mouth and drank again. "Listen, what happened? It wasn't any accident, was it? I knew that much when the two county boys said they had instructions to bring me here."

"No, it wasn't an accident."

"Somebody set it on purpose."

"That's right."

"Who?"

"A fortyish bald guy who so far doesn't have a name. We went down to have a talk with you around nine-thirty last night, and we got there in time to see him running away along the beach—but not in time to do anything about saving your place. The guy got away and we haven't found him yet."

The left side of Dancer's mouth began to tic. He looked at me. "Is this the guy you mentioned to me yesterday—Paige's friend?"

I nodded, and Quartermain said, "You claimed yesterday not to know him, that you'd never seen him before. Does that still hold?"

"Yeah, it holds. I don't know anybody who looks like that, and I don't know why the son of a bitch would want to set fire to my goddamn house."

"We can answer that one. He wanted to destroy any and all copies of *The Dead and the Dying* that you might have had."

Dancer stared at him grimly. "So that's it."

"That's it."

"How do you know?"

I said, "Paige's copy of the book was stolen from my cottage at the Beachwood, probably just before that guy went to your place. And when he went there, he took a can of gasoline with him. He didn't want to take the time to search through all of your belongings, and maybe miss something in the bargain; the simplest, surest way was for him to fire the house."

"If you'd been there," Quartermain put in, "he might have seen to it that you went up along with it."

Dancer said "Jesus" almost reverently.

"There's something damned important in that book, Dancer, something important enough to create a motive for murder. The key to everything is in that book, in *why* it's important."

"I don't understand that, any of it. A book of mine, a potboiler paperback crime novel twenty years old—how could a thing like that be important enough to anybody to cause murder and arson?"

"That's why you're here: to help us find out."

"I can't even remember the thing."

"None of it?"

"No, none of it."

Quartermain's mouth tightened. "The bald man must have thought you could. If you'd been home last night, you'd very likely be dead now because of it."

"It's a farce," Dancer said, and shook his head numbly. "This whole thing is a farce, for Christ's sake. I can't tell you anything." With a kind of mute appeal in his eyes, he looked at me again. "Listen, after you came to see me yesterday, I was bugged about the book and I went to my shelves to dig out a copy. But I didn't have one. I didn't have one. The bastard fired the house for nothing. For *nothing*. I didn't even have a god-

160

damn copy of it!" He laughed abruptly—humorless and savagely bitter.

Quartermain asked, "Not even a manuscript carbon?"

"No. I looked for that, too; it wasn't among my other papers. I don't know what happened to it. It might have gotten thrown out; my ex-wife was a great one for throwing things out."

"Goddamn it, can't you remember *any* of the book? At least what type of crime, besides murder, it dealt with?"

"I'm lucky I can remember my name this morning."

I said, "The lead's name was Johnny Sunderland—a Korean War vet with a game leg. He came home to San Francisco and got mixed up with a couple of women, one of them named . . . Dina, I think. There were some hoods involved and two hundred thousand dollars. Sunderland and this Dina pulled some kind of double-cross, apparently, and tried to run off with the money."

"That sounds like the plot of half the crappy crime books I did in the fifties. Look, I used to crank those things out in a week or two, first draft with minor revisions. I put titles on them, but the publishers always changed the titles; half the time they edited the stuff and changed character names, too. The gimpy Korean vet sounds vaguely familiar, but I can't place him in any kind of situation. I'm sorry as hell—don't you think I want to help you find out what this is all about, who that bald bastard is?—but I just can't remember."

Quartermain got up and began pacing off his frustrated anger, and then stopped moving just as abruptly and said to Dancer, "Have you got any idea where we might get a copy of the book now, this morning?"

"An old paperback like that—no, I don't have any idea."

"You were living in this area when you wrote it, weren't you?"

"I moved out here from New York in 1950."

"Is it possible you gave copies to friends at that time? You did have copies then, didn't you?"

"Christ, I don't know. I always try to get copies of my published stuff, but there were some books the publishers didn't bother sending and I couldn't locate; *The Dead and the Dying* might have been one of them. If I did have copies, I may have given some away, but nobody except a collector would have kept the damned thing around for twenty years, and I never knew any collectors."

"All right, then," Quartermain said thinly. "Let's forget about the book for the time being and talk about Walter Paige."

"What about Paige?"

"You had trouble with him at one time, didn't you?"

"Trouble—?"

"Words about something, bad feelings, a fight."

Dancer hesitated, and then sighed in a resigned way. "All right, yeah, we had some words once."

"What about?"

"A chick I was seeing at that time. He tried to move in on her one night and I didn't like it. I told him to lay off and he told me to go screw, and it looked for a time as if we might take a few swings at one another. We were both pretty drunk. But it was at the Mount Royal and some of the others in the group broke it up. Keith Tarrant was there, I think. Is he the one who told you about it?"

I said, "Why didn't you mention this yesterday?"

"It didn't amount to anything, and I didn't think it was particularly relevant. Besides, I didn't want to put ideas in your head."

"Who was the girl?" Quartermain asked him.

"Rose Davis."

"Does she still live in this area?"

"No, she moved back east a couple of years ago."

"Where back east?"

"St. Louis. She got married to some guy from there."

"Did Paige leave her alone after that one night?"

"If he didn't, Rose never said anything to me about it."

"Then you didn't have any more trouble with Paige?"

"No."

"Did you ever hear of an alleged attempt by Paige to attack Robin Lomax?"

Dancer frowned. "You mean a rape thing?"

"That's what I mean."

"No, I never heard of anything like that."

"Does it sound like something Paige might have done?"

"Not really. He was glib and smooth and virile as hell; he could talk most broads out of their pants with a little effort, and he was never lacking for pussy as far as I could see. A guy like that doesn't usually blow his cool enough to attempt rape." He frowned again. "Did Robin tell you that Paige tried to attack her?"

"Her husband told us."

"You think they're involved in Paige's death—this business with my book?"

"Anything is possible at this point," Quartermain said. "Did Paige seem to be hot for Robin six years ago?"

"No hotter than he was for every other woman he met. But she was pretty thick with Lomax back then; I doubt if she ever gave Paige a tumble."

"Was she much of a drinker?"

"Yeah, she could put it away."

"Could she hold it?"

"Fair. I've seen her juiced a few times, before she married Lomax and became a Miss Junior League."

"Then she might have gotten drunk enough, if she'd had a fight with Lomax, say, to go out with Paige?"

Dancer shrugged. "I suppose so."

"Lomax used to join your little group once in a while?"

"Robin dragged him along a couple of times. He didn't seem to approve of us—a stuffy bastard."

"How did he get along with Paige?"

"They seemed to tolerate one another."

"No trouble over Robin?"

"Not that I know about."

"When Paige moved away, were either of the Lomaxes still attending your group sessions?"

"Sure, they both were."

"No animosity, no strained feelings toward Paige?"

"If there were, I can't remember them."

"You'd think there would be if Paige had tried to rape her, wouldn't you?" The question was rhetorical; he followed it immediately with: "Tell me something about Brad Winestock."

"Like what?"

"How well did he know Paige six years ago?"

"As well as the rest of us, I guess. Winestock used to join the group with his sister once in a while, just like Lomax used to come with Robin."

"He never seemed thick with Paige?"

"If you mean buddy-buddy, no."

"When was the last time you saw Winestock?"

"A month, two months; he drives a bread truck, and I saw him here in Cypress Bay one morning and we said hello."

"Just that? You didn't talk about anything?"

"The weather, maybe. Why all the interest in Winestock now?"

"He was murdered last night," Quartermain told him flatly.

Dancer blinked a couple of times, absorbing that. Then he said "God" and put the coffee cup down on the desk. "Does Beverly know yet?"

"Yes, she knows."

"Ah Christ! And I thought I had it rough today." His throat worked painfully. "Who did it? The bald man again?"

"Maybe; we can't be sure yet. But Winestock was mixed up with the bald man, and with Walter Paige. He spent part of the afternoon with the guy yesterday, and Paige called him up on the phone a few weeks ago and had at least one meeting with him. His sister thinks they were planning something, some kind of crime, something to do with that book of yours. We came down a little hard on Winestock last night, and then left him sweating; I figured maybe he'd lead us to the bald man. But he slipped the tail I had on him and vanished. A Highway Patrol unit found him out at Spanish—"

The telephone bell, as shrill as the cry of a loon, cut Quartermain off. He went to the desk and caught up the handset and listened for a time, not contributing much; then he thanked the caller, replaced the receiver, and said to us, "County people at Jamesburg. The Nunnally woman confirmed that you spent the night with her, Dancer—reluctantly, but she confirmed it. She says you weren't out of her sight more than ten minutes at any time."

Dancer did not say anything. His eyebrows were humped in a V over the bridge of his nose, and there was sweat on his splotched gray face, and you could see that he was trying to think on something or other and having difficulty with it because of the hangover dullness of his mind. Finally he said, with slow deliberateness as if testing the words and his memory, "Anita Hartman."

Quartermain looked at him blankly. "What?"

"Anita Hartman," Dancer said again. "An old lady, a pioneer type, who used to live in Cypress Bay. I think she died two or three years ago."

The blankness congealed into a frown. "Sure, I remember her; she was something of an institution in this area. What about her?"

"She was trying to start up this combination art and historical society back in the late fifties—a museum or something for the storage and preservation of artistic memorabilia relating to Cypress Bay and environs, supposed to date back to the time of the Spanish possession. I don't know why she was interested in an old pulp hack, but she found out I was a local writer and came to see me. She wanted me to donate some of my papers to this society of hers—she was seeing other writers and artists in the area and getting them to donate stuff and she wanted to include me. I guess I was a little flattered and so I said all right and gave her two or three boxes of stuff. She said she wanted all future papers, too, but the project fell through and I never heard from her again. I'd forgotten all about her until just now."

Quartermain and I were both on our feet, and there was a kind of electric tenseness in the air. He said, "You think there may have been copies of *The Dead and the Dying* among those papers of yours, is that it?"

"Not copies—the manuscript carbon. I don't know exactly what was in the boxes I gave her, but I'm pretty sure, now that I remember it, that most of the stuff was manuscript carbons and notes on some of the books and stories I'd done since 1950."

I said to Quartermain, "Do you know what happened, after she died, to all the memorabilia Anita Hartman had collected?"

"Hell yes. She willed it to the city of Cypress Bay, with the stipulation that it be stored safely until such time as it could be used to start or implement a local historical art society. There's been a lot of renewed interest in our local heritage of late, and a community group with city sanction and funding is in the process of creating a Cypress Bay Historical Museum of Art and Literature. Not long ago they bought an old schoolhouse on Gutierrez Avenue and have begun to restore it. All of Anita Hartman's collection, and other donations, are stored in the basement until restoration is complete and they can sort it and arrange displays."

"Is there a custodian, someone to let us in?"

"No, not yet; it's still a volunteer group and they won't get somebody in there until it's opened to the public. It's kept locked."

"Who would have the key?"

"I'm not sure. The head of the group, probably. I think that's John Benjamin, but I'd better— Wait a minute! Keith Tarrant belongs to the group; he got them the schoolhouse property through his real-estate office. He'd have a key; sure he would."

We pulled Dancer up from his chair—there was the chance we might need his help in combing the schoolhouse basement, if not in further explanations, were we to locate the manuscript of *The Dead and the Dying*—and hurried the hell out of there . . .

Eighteen

The real-estate office which Keith Tarrant maintained in Cypress Bay was located on Newberry Road, just inside the northern city limits. We went there directly from the City Hall because it was close and because it seemed reasonable that Tarrant would keep a schoolhouse key there rather than at his Carmel Valley home; even if he had not as yet come in, the secretary he had told me about would more than likely have opened the office for Monday morning business.

Quartermain brought the car into the curb in front of the place—a pine-shaded, ivy-draped, one-story frame structure—and there were lights on inside and a sign in the glass front door reading *Please Come In*. The three of us crossed the sun-and-shade-dappled sidewalk and entered; a chunky brunette in her middle forties was sitting behind a dove-gray metal desk and doing something with a sheaf of papers. She was not alone. On the near side of the functionally appointed room, in one of those round, modernistic comfort chairs, sat Bianca Tarrant.

She wore an emerald-green, lightweight pants suit, and her auburn hair had a sleek, carefully brushed appearance; there was artfully applied make-up around her eyes and on her

168

mouth, and some to soften the tone of the sepia freckles across the bridge of her nose. She looked poised and assured—and yet, you could tell she was suffering a hangover. It was in her violet-rimmed eyes and in the faint pouches beneath them that the make-up could not quite conceal. Nothing like the hangover Dancer was suffering, but a hangover nonetheless.

She looked at us as we came in, and surprise parted her lips and put faint furrows in the pale smoothness of her forehead. A little uncertainly, she stood up; her eyes moved restlessly from one to the other of us: three haggard, unshaven, middle-aged men, two in rumpled suits, one in slacks and a sports shirt. Not exactly a trio to inspire ease or a sense of normalcy. She took a step toward us and then stopped, still uncertain.

Quartermain said, "Good morning, Mrs. Tarrant. Is your husband here?"

"Why . . . no, not at the moment, Chief." Her voice was husky and cultured, with none of the odd intensity that had inflected her words to me the day before. "He left about fifteen minutes ago, to see a client briefly. He should be back any time now; we're attending a luncheon in Monterey."

"Do you know if he keeps a key here to the old schoolhouse on Gutierrez?"

Her frown deepened. "I don't know, I suppose he does." She made a half-turn toward the secretary's desk. "Margot . . . ?"

"Yes," the brunette said. "It should be in his office."

"Would you get it, please?" Quartermain asked her.

"Of course." She stood up and went through an unmarked door at the rear of the room.

Bianca Tarrant said, "Is something wrong at the museum?"

"No, it's nothing like that."

Her gaze strayed to Dancer. "Russ, we heard on the radio this morning about the fire. I'm so sorry. How did it happen?"

"Somebody set it deliberately."

"Oh no . . ."

Quartermain said, "I have a few questions, if you wouldn't mind, Mrs. Tarrant."

"Questions?"

"About Walter Paige."

She shifted the weight of her body uncomfortably, looked at me, looked away, looked at me again. "Because of what I said to you yesterday?" she asked in a soft, nervous voice. "Well, you know, I . . . was a little high yesterday; Keith and I had been drinking quite a bit. I'm sorry about . . . well, I suppose I did act somewhat strangely, didn't I?"

"Somewhat," I said.

"It was just that I was a little high," she said. "I knew Walt Paige six years ago, and it was such a shock to learn that he had been murdered . . ." She cleared her throat. "Have you found out who killed him yet?"

"Not yet."

"Do you have any idea who it was?"

"Possibly."

"Who?"

"Do you know a bald man in his forties, heavy-set, dark?"

"I don't believe so. Is . . . he the one you suspect?"

"We're trying to find him," Quartermain said. "You and Paige were friends, is that correct?"

"Yes. We were friends."

"But you hadn't seen him in six years?"

"No. No, I hadn't."

"Did you know he had come back to Cypress Bay?"

"No. He . . . didn't try to get in touch with us or anything."

"But he did, Mrs. Tarrant."

"What?"

"He called your husband several weeks ago and tried to rent a vacant store here in Cypress Bay; your husband turned him down. You didn't know about that?"

170

"Keith didn't tell me, no." Her hands moved against one another like furtive lovers. "I can't imagine Walt trying to rent a vacant store—unless he was planning to move back to this area. Why did my husband turn him down?"

"He said he didn't care for Paige, that Paige was not the type of man he cared to have for a neighbor. Why would he say that if the three of you were friendly six years ago?"

"I don't know. He . . . I always thought he and Walt were friendly. He's never said any differently to me."

"What was his reaction to Paige's death?"

"Well, he was shocked, naturally. Just as I was." She moistened her lips. "We were both shocked, too, when we heard this morning about poor Brad Winestock. Does that have any connection with what happened to Walt?"

"It might. We're not certain just yet."

The door at the rear of the room opened and the brunette reappeared. "The schoolhouse key doesn't seem to be in Mr. Tarrant's key file," she said. "He usually keeps it there, but he was at the schoolhouse on Friday, and he may still have it with him."

"He'll be back shortly, you said?" Quartermain asked Bianca Tarrant.

"Yes, any minute now."

She did not seem to want to do any more talking; she returned to her chair and sat down and opened a large handbag on the floor beside it and made a project out of lighting a mentholated cigarette. Her hands were agitated. Smoke fanned out of her nostrils and from between her lips, and she watched it eddy and swirl as if the nebulous patterns held a great fascination for her; she did not look at any of us.

The brunette sat down, wearing a bewildered expression, and Quartermain took Dancer's arm and moved him over near the door. I followed them. Quartermain said sotto voce, "What about Paige and Mrs. Tarrant, Dancer? Was there ever anything between them?"

"Hell, I can't tell you if there was or wasn't. Paige didn't brag up his conquests, and if the two of them were playing around, they sure as Christ weren't talking about it in company."

"She's acting guilty as hell about something," Quartermain said darkly. "What and why, if there was nothing between them?"

Neither Dancer nor I had any answers for that—but even if we had had any, we would not have had time to put voice to them. There was movement out on the sidewalk, and the glass-paneled door opened and Keith Tarrant came briskly into the office. He stopped when he saw the three of us standing there, glanced over at his wife, and then gave us a wan smile. If he was also suffering a hangover, he did not show it; his eyes were clear and his round face was smooth and line-free. He wore tan slacks and a soft light-brown sports jacket and a beige tie—moneyed attire.

"Gentlemen," he said.

"Hello, Keith," Quartermain said, and Dancer and I nodded.

"You all look like you've had a rough night." His smile went away. "You especially, Russ. A damned shame, what happened to your place last night."

"Yeah," Dancer said.

"Well—I gather you're waiting to see me?"

"We are," Quartermain told him. "We'd like to have the key to the old schoolhouse on Gutierrez Avenue."

"The museum?" Tarrant looked puzzled. "What would you want in there?"

"There are some things in the basement we'd like to look through. Specifically, Anita Hartman's donation."

"May I ask why?"

"We're looking for boxes of papers and such Dancer here

gave Miss Hartman a few years ago. There may be a manuscript carbon of *The Dead and the Dying* among them."

"Oh, so that's it," Tarrant said. "The book *does* have something to do with Paige's death, then?"

"We think it might. And with what happened to Dancer's place, and with the murder of Brad Winestock."

"God, is all of that interconnected?"

"It would seem to be."

Tarrant looked at Dancer. "Russ, you wrote the book; why do you need the manuscript carbon?"

"I wrote it twenty years ago," Dancer told him. "Can you remember details of what you were doing twenty years ago?"

"Yes, I see what you mean. Well, the key is in my briefcase, in the trunk of my car. I'll get it for you right away."

"Would you mind coming over to the schoolhouse with us, Keith?" Quartermain asked.

"I guess not—but Bianca and I have a luncheon engagement in Monterey. Do you really need me?"

"I'd like to discuss some things with you, and it would save time if we talked over there. You can bring your wife along and leave for Monterey from the schoolhouse."

"Just as you say, then," Tarrant agreed. He went over to where his wife was sitting. "Bianca?"

"Yes," she said, "all right."

She had gotten the nervousness out of her voice, and her words were controlled. She stood up and Tarrant put his arm around her shoulders and told the brunette that if there were any calls, he expected to be back in Cypress Bay by four o'clock. Then the five of us filed out, and the Tarrants went down to where his Chrysler was parked a short distance away. A few seconds later Quartermain pulled out to lead the way to Gutierrez Avenue.

The schoolhouse was a simple Early California building, complete with a bell tower atop its canted tile roof—an old and stern and vaguely melancholy structure with time-scarred adobe walls; but the bell tower was freshly painted and you could see the big iron bell within gleaming dully in the warm morning sunlight, as if recently polished.

We parked directly in front, and Tarrant pulled up behind us and got out and opened the trunk for his briefcase. Sparrows and blackbirds chattered in the surrounding trees and shrubs, but there was nonetheless a hushed quality about the school-house—as if a place that had once been the dispensary of simple knowledge commanded a certain solemnity and respect from all living things. It was a fitting location, I thought, for the Cypress Bay Historical Museum of Art and Literature.

Quartermain went to the Chrysler and said something to Tarrant as he was about to open the door for his wife. I saw him frown slightly, and then shrug, and then lean in to speak to her; I knew Quartermain had asked that Mrs. Tarrant remain in the car—that he wanted to ask his questions of Tarrant without her being present. She stayed where she was, and Quartermain and Tarrant came up to join Dancer and me on a packed-earth path leading through the grounds.

The schoolhouse's front entrance was set into a recessed arch—heavy, triangular-hinged double doors with an old-fashioned bronze latch in one of them. Tarrant used his key, and the door swung inward to reveal a cool mustiness and thick, mass-shadowed gloom.

"We've had the electricity turned on for some time now," he said. "I'll get the lights."

He stepped inside and moved away to the left and moments later fluorescent tubes suspended from the ceiling flickered like strobe lights and then came on brightly. I saw as we entered that a considerable amount of labor had been expended by the volunteer citizens' group. Walls had been knocked down and partitions erected, and there was scaffolding and an array of ladders

174

and sawhorses and paint canvases and hand tools strewn about the dusty floor.

Tarrant indicated an archway across the enlarged main room. "The basement stairs are through there, in the back. I'll take you down, if you want."

Quartermain nodded. "We can do our talking on the way."

"Just what was it you wanted to discuss with me, Chief?"

"I'm going to get a little personal, but it can't be avoided. Just how well did your wife know Walter Paige six years ago?"

Tarrant gave him a sharp-eyed look. "Why do you ask that?"

"She seems to be taking his death pretty hard—a man she hadn't seen in six years and supposedly knew only in a casual way at that time."

"Supposedly? Just what are you getting at?"

"The truth, I hope."

"Are you trying to intimate Bianca is the woman Paige had in his bed just before he was killed? That you think she had something to do with his death?"

"I don't think anything at this point. I'm only trying to find out why she's so obviously emotionally upset by Paige's murder. Are you going to tell me you haven't noticed, Keith?"

Tarrant started to say something, appeared to change his mind, and pressed his lips together in a thin, tight line.

Quartermain said, "Well?"

"Oh Christ, all right. I've noticed."

"Can you explain why?"

"I think I can." Tarrant stopped as we passed under the rear arch into another work-littered chamber, and looked pointedly at Dancer. "Will you hold what I say in confidence, Russ?"

"I do enough tale-telling on paper," Dancer said.

Tarrant took a long breath as we began moving again, toward a short hallway at the far end of the chamber. "Six years ago," he said, "Bianca was . . . attracted to Paige. Just one of

175

those things that happen: a powerful physical attraction. I saw it almost immediately, and instead of trying to delude myself that there was nothing to it, I confronted her with it. She tried to deny it, but I managed to get the truth out of her; Paige wasn't averse to dating other men's wives, God knows, and she had let him talk her into a meeting. I told her that if she wanted to keep that date, if she wanted Paige that much, I wouldn't stand in her way. She could have him if he was what she really wanted, but she had better make up her mind right away. If she chose to sacrifice our marriage for a love affair that couldn't possibly last, all right, but she would have to make a quick, clean break with me. I wouldn't stand for an affair."

Quartermain said, "And she chose you—your marriage."

"That's right. Putting it all on the line was the wisest thing I could have done; otherwise she would probably have let him seduce her on that date she'd made."

"You're certain nothing like that happened between them?"

"Yes, I'm certain. I watched her carefully after she'd made her announced choice. She was faithful to me and to her word; I would have known if she wasn't."

"She said she thought you and Paige were friends; she was surprised when we told her about Paige's phone call five weeks ago, and why you turned him down on the store rental. Why would she think you were friendly after what happened—or almost happened?"

"If I had shown hatred or animosity toward Paige, made an issue of my real feelings toward the man, it might well have driven her away from me—or at least have established a wall between us. But by pretending I was still friendly to Paige, that I bore no grudges, I maintained the status quo in our relationship and there were no difficulties. Then Paige left Cypress Bay and I thought he'd gone for good. When he called me about the vacant newsstand, I naturally refused him and I naturally did not tell

176

Bianca about his presence in this area again. You can understand that."

"Uh-huh. But six years is a lot of water under the bridge. If
she hadn't seen him in that length of time, why is she so upset
over his death?"

We were in the hallway now, and Tarrant stopped before a
heavy door set into the right-hand wall. He unlocked it with a
second key, pushed it open, and reached along the wall inside to
click a toggle switch. Pale light cut through the blackness to reveal a set of railed wooden steps leading downward. He began to
descend, speaking over his shoulder. "Bianca is an emotional
woman, Chief. Even though she realized six years ago and
knows now that an affair with Paige would have been the
gravest mistake of her life, I think she still feels or felt a certain
something for him. I hate to admit that, but it seems to be a fact.
And when she learned he was dead and dead so violently here in
Cypress Bay, she was understandably upset by it. I suppose if
you were throwing questions at her like you've been throwing
them at me, she became flustered and began acting guilty of
something or other. That's simply the way she is."

We reached the bottom of the steps. The basement was
stuffy and smelled of dust and dry rot, as all basements in tem-
perate climates seem to. Huge and low-ceilinged, it was jammed
with boxes and crates and paper-wrapped pictures in frames
and rolled canvases and cloth-covered sculptures and miscella-
neous pottery and two very old typewriters which had probably
belonged to some local early-century writer.

Tarrant took us off to the right and indicated a great conglomerate of items, most of them cardboard and wooden boxes
of various sizes, stacked apart from the rest of the accumulation
of art and memorabilia. "That's the Anita Hartman donation,"
he said. "We haven't had the chance to do any cataloguing of it
as yet; we've barely begun cataloguing anything, as a matter of
fact."

177

"Okay," Quartermain said. "We'll take over from here."

"No more questions?"

"For now, no."

"For now," Tarrant said. "I suppose that means you'll be around to see Bianca and me again."

"I don't know, Keith. I hope not."

"So do I. Good luck with your hunting—here and elsewhere." He turned brusquely and left the three of us standing there and went up the steps and was gone.

Looking sourly at the conglomerate, Dancer said, "Where the hell do we start? The stuff I gave the old lady could be any place in this mess."

"One of us on each end of the pile and one in the middle," Quartermain told him. "Let's get busy."

We got busy. We moved sculptures and paintings out of the way and went to work on the crates and boxes. None of us said anything; further talk would have been a waste of time. Punctuated only by the rustle of papers and cardboard and the scrape of wood, the silence was grim and tense. The stuffiness became oppressive, and sweat poured freely down my cheeks and into the soiled collar of my shirt; I could smell the sour, unhygienic odor of it on my body. The fine dust we continually stirred up aggravated my lungs and created a dry cough that combined with Quartermain's labored, almost asthmatic breathing and Dancer's occasional sick belches to form a kind of consumptive symphony.

Twenty unproductive minutes had gone by, and we had sifted through maybe two-thirds of the Anita Hartman collection, when Dancer pulled out a heavy cardboard box and opened it and said thickly, "This is it—one of them."

Quartermain and I moved quickly to his side, and Dancer was down on his knees pulling papers out of the box. "I think I gave her two cartons," he said. "I hope to God it's in this one. I hope to God it's in *one* of them."

178

Near the bottom he uncovered several rubber-band-bound book manuscript carbons, rumpled and yellowed with age. He shuffled through the pages of four and discarded them while we watched sweating, then he began to go through a fifth with the title *You Can't Run Away from Murder* centered on the facing page, and after a moment he stopped shuffling the pages and turned his face up to me. "What did you say the lead's name was?"

"Johnny Sunderland."

The beginnings of a savage smile touched his mouth. "This is it, then. The publishers changed the title, the way they used to do. But Johnny Sunderland—this is it, all right."

The rubber banding crumbled as he pulled it off and began to scan the manuscript pages, his lips moving silently as he read the words and sought to refamiliarize himself with the book. Quartermain and I said nothing, waiting grimly, knowing that the answer was in there and that we would have it in a matter of minutes, dreading the knowledge just a little because of the kind of thing it surely had to be.

And it was that kind of thing, all right. Dancer's memory yielded the book's plot after two chapters, and he was able to pinpoint then the exact location of what we were looking for.

A bank robbery.

Just as simple as that: a bank robbery.

We spent three or four additional minutes urgently talking it over, making certain; then we got out of the basement and out of the schoolhouse in search of the nearest telephone—running all the way.

Nineteen

I was sitting in a place called the Old Bavarian Inn, a combination café and German-style beer hall located directly across Balboa Street from the vacant newsstand Walter Paige had tried to rent in Cypress Bay. I had been there for close to an hour, in one of the high-backed wooden booths next to the curtained front window—burning my lungs with too many cigarettes and tightening my nerves dangerously with too much coffee and no food at all; watching the dark and cobblestoned little alley that bisected the block next to the newsstand, waiting for something to happen, wondering if something *would* happen or if the balding guy had abandoned the thing at the last minute because of the heavy risk factor.

There was a thin, cold-hot sweat on my forehead and my eyes felt inflamed and my thoughts were sluggish and somewhere along the line I had developed a sore throat; I had pushed myself to just about the limit of my physical endurance, and unless I got some tension-free rest pretty soon, there would be physiological hell to pay. But the tension would not abate, and I would not be able to sleep until something happened or did not

180

happen across the street and seven doors to the south: the Cypress Bay National Exchange Bank.

We still did not know much of the background yet, but the *what* and the *how* had all been there in *The Dead and the Dying*. The robbery had only been important in the book because it was the source of the two hundred thousand dollars which the protagonist, Johnny Sunderland, and his mistress had later stolen from the four men who had pulled the holdup; Dancer had spent only a chapter on the robbery, and that in flashback. But the plan was a relatively clever one, and he had related its execution in detail.

In the book, one of the holdup men had once been an electrician who was familiar with both the small California town of Cliffside and with the town's major banking operation, the Cliffside Savings and Loan. On the day of the robbery he was the first of the team to enter the bank—dressed in a business suit and posing as a new and well-to-do arrival in the community. He had asked to see the president of the bank about a loan, and had been granted the audience. Once alone with the president, the electrician had produced a gun and forced the president to conduct him downstairs into the basement area where the bank's alarm system was located.

The electrician had rendered the alarms inoperable, as well as all phone lines, and had then taken the president back upstairs into the bank proper. Waiting there were two of the remaining three members of the gang, pretending to be customers and fussing with deposit slips. At gunpoint they had taken over the bank, locking the door and pulling the shades over the front window; teller's cages and the vault were cleaned out for the exaggerated sum of two hundred thousand, employees and four unfortunate citizens were made to lie on the floor at the rear of the building. Then the three men had made good their exit.

Dancer's cleverness went one step further here: there was a

vacant bakery located half a block from the bank and which bordered on an alley leading through to the next parallel street. Some weeks prior to the holdup date, one member of the gang had managed to rent the bakery under an assumed name; on the day of the robbery and just prior to it, he had let himself into the vacant store with his key, leaving the alley door unlocked and ajar. When the other three reached the alley, they checked to make certain it was empty and then entered and began stripping off certain simple items of disguise such as dark glasses and wigs; then, as they passed the partially open bakery door, they stuffed the items plus the guns they had used in the holdup into the satchel containing the bank's money. One of them opened the door, tossed the satchel inside to the waiting fourth man, and the trio then continued through to the parallel street. The maneuver in the alley required no more than a few seconds.

There was as a result no need for a swift and dangerous getaway, along roads which soon would be blocked by local, county, and state police. They had no incriminating evidence in their possession—no money and no weapons—and they looked somewhat different from the men who had held up the bank as well; even if, by some chance, they had later been stopped for questioning, which they had not been, there was nothing at all to link them with the crime. They simply split up, on foot, wandered around town for a while like any other resident or tourist, and then met later at one of two motels they were utilizing in a nearby city. The two hundred thousand remained inside the vacant bakery overnight; the following morning it had been transported, in a cardboard box, by the fourth man to a third Cliffside motel. After a week to allow things to cool down, the four left the area separately and met in San Francisco to divide the swag; and that was where Johnny Sunderland had come in.

Dancer told Quartermain and me that he had gotten the robbery idea from an electrician friend of his, in 1953, who had helped to install the basement alarm system in the Cypress Bay

National Exchange Bank. Caper books were not much in vogue in the early fifties, and so Dancer had simply "thrown away" the holdup idea in his contrivance of *The Dead and the Dying*; and it was because he had, because it played such a small part in the actual plot of the book, that he had not been able to remember it these twenty years later.

The way it seemed to us, Paige or the balding guy or Winestock—most probably Paige—had happened upon Dancer's book, had read it, and had known or remembered enough about Cypress Bay to recognize both that the village was the model for the fictional Cliffside and that the Cypress Bay National Exchange Bank was the model for the fictional Cliffside Savings and Loan. Some simple if discreet checking had revealed that the National Exchange Bank was still housed in the same building as in 1953, and that its alarm system—comprised today of silent alarms and hidden television cameras—was still located and still vulnerable in its basement. And once they were able, by luck or design, to obtain a vacant store bordering on an alley near the bank, they had the perfect blueprint for an actual holdup.

Now, with knowledge of the robbery and with simple hindsight, I could see the various facts which Quartermain and I might have put together *without* the book to determine that a bank holdup was the answer—the pieces I had known were there earlier, but which I had not been able to separate and correlate from all the other pieces. There was the vacant newsstand and its location in downtown Cypress Bay; we could not have known exactly why it was important without *The Dead and the Dying*, but if I had noted yesterday which business establishments were located in the general vicinity as well as immediately surrounding the newsstand—or if Quartermain had made an association between the proximity of the store and the bank —we would have, with the other facts, been able to guess the truth. The other facts: today's date—the first of May, the first of the month—payday for a large number of local employees; the banners I had seen on Saturday announcing the beginning of the Sentinel Hill Professional Golf Classic, a major tournament which always attracts golf buffs and tourists equipped with traveler's checks and personal checks that require cashing; the combination of those two facts to make a third: the necessity of a local bank such as the National Exchange to have a large amount of available cash on hand—more cash than it would normally keep and thus a boodle big enough to make the time and expense of a complicated holdup worthwhile; the fact that at least three men—Paige, the balding man, Winestock—were involved, which tended to rule out a large number of major-profit crimes, since such ploys as kidnapping and extortion would hardly require more than one or two principals; the fact that in a small community like Cypress Bay, a bank would be the *only* source of enough money to make feasible a plot involving three or more men and the subsequent split of the take; and, finally, Judith Paige's comment in my office on Friday that her husband had told her he would be in Cypress Bay not only until Sunday but until "late Monday afternoon," which confirmed the day and approximate time of the robbery and bore out our feelings of urgency.

Quartermain's frantic check with the president of the National Exchange Bank, following our reading of the carbon at the schoolhouse, had determined that until that moment everything was perfectly normal. The robbery, then, had either been aborted or they were waiting until later in the day—any time up until six o'clock, since the bank stayed open late on the first of the month. Quartermain had had to make the choice, assuming there had been no abortion of the plan, of whether or not to allow the execution of it.

He could have arrested the balding man as soon as he showed his face, and raided the vacant newsstand immediately, and put the arm on anyone asking to see the bank president who was not known to him; but since no crime had actually been committed, the only charge which could be made was that of conspiracy—and a conviction on that score was tenuous at best. And there was no concrete evidence linking the balding man or any other member of the potential holdup team to the deaths of Paige or Brad Winestock; if neither murder weapon could be located, the State would have nothing but supposition and circumstantial evidence—and a relatively minor arson complaint against the balding guy—with which to go to court.

In view of that, Quartermain had grimly decided to let the robbery take place if still scheduled. He had explained the situation to the bank president and had assured the man that every precaution would be taken to circumvent any potential danger; the president had agreed, although reluctantly, to the Chief's wishes. Quartermain had immediately delegated three armed men in plainclothes to the National Exchange Bank, to pose as examiners and employees. They had orders to take instantaneous action if the holdup commenced before Quartermain had mobilized the balance of a local, county, and state trap force, or if it appeared in any way that harm would befall a private citizen. The risk factor was still prominent—you can't anticipate the unforeseen—but with each bank employee apprised beforehand of what might happen so that no one would become heroic, the danger was not great. And since the blueprint called for disposal of money and weapons and disguises into the newsstand, and the success of that part of the plan depended on both time and inconspicuousness, the holdup men could not afford any shooting, any trouble at all. They would be very careful, and the bank people would be very careful; as long as fate stayed out of it, there would be no problems.

As covertly as possible, Lieutenant Favor—returned from Monterey—and several other men dressed in plainclothes had been sent to predetermined stations on Balboa and Pine streets. County and Highway Patrol units were on standby at each of the Cypress Bay exits, and others were deployed in the vicinity if needed. And then the waiting had begun.

I would have liked to have been an active participant myself, but there were limits to my involvement as a private citizen and this was one of them; all Quartermain could do was to tell me about the Old Bavarian Inn, and its rear garden entrance, and allow me to assume a passive spectator's role. Dancer had wanted to come along, too, but Quartermain had told him no as a precautionary measure and because Dancer was still hangover-sick and badly agitated and in need of a couple of shots of pure oxygen; he had been escorted, grumbling, to the local hospital.

So I had come alone to the Old Bavarian Inn, and had sat here alone to wait it out, and now I wondered again where Quartermain was and if all the arrangements had been made and if his men in their deployment were cool enough to maintain the illusion of complete normalcy. And how long it would be before the balding man showed, if he was going to show; and if their plan was already in operation, as I knew it could be; and if Quartermain's trap would spring as silently and as bloodlessly as he anticipated . . .

I lit another cigarette off the butt of one smoldering in the ashtray, and coughed, and wiped some of the sweat off my forehead. Sporadically, people came in and went out of the dark, beam-ceilinged room—and boisterous laughter and the clink of beer steins filtered in from a pair of tables jammed with tourists in the grape-arbored rear garden. Outside on Balboa, passers-by were few and desultory past the alley entrance and the newsstand.

Two-twenty.

This is the ideal time, if they're going through with it, I thought. Midafternoon lull. People sunning on the beach or sitting in the park or walking by the sea, people napping in motel rooms and hotel rooms, people drinking beer or eating ice cream

186

in places like this one. Any time from now until three o'clock. After that, the tourists go shopping again and the kids are out of school and the housewives run errands and taxi service, and the breadwinners of both sexes begin getting off work and heading for—

Two men in the alley, walking toward Balboa.

I leaned hard against the window, working new sweat off my forehead and blinking heavily to clear strain-shadows from my vision. Two men wearing business suits, one short and thick-set and carrying a large valise and wearing a broad-brimmed hat. A hat—in this weather, in Cypress Bay? The balding guy? He was still in shadow and I could not see his face clearly. The other one was tall and spare, light hair in a brush cut.

They kept on walking, briskly, and then they stopped, and where they stopped was at the padlocked alley door to the newsstand. The thin one used a key on the lock and removed it and pulled the door open and went inside and closed the door after himself; it was difficult to be certain from my angle, but it did not look as if he had closed it all the way. The one in the hat came forward, out of the alley, and stopped to squint at the bright flush of the sun.

It was the balding man, all right.

Even with the hat I had no trouble recognizing him, and I thought: So they're going through with it, the stupid, cocky bastards are going through with it after all. They've got a guy inside already, one I don't know or I would have noticed him entering the bank—three of them then, a skeleton crew, but that's all they really need. I let out a soft breath and felt some of the tenseness flow out of me, some but not all because the trap was yet to spring and a lot of things could go wrong, a hell of a lot of things could go wrong.

The balding man took a pair of wide-lensed and very dark sunglasses from the breast pocket of his suit jacket and put them on; then he pivoted and started down the sidewalk to the south. He passed the six storefronts and turned into the National Exchange Bank without hesitation—a professional man going to work.

Four minutes later the amber-colored shades in the front window and front door of the bank went down, and I knew the door had been locked as well.

I had not seen anyone enter the National Exchange except the balding guy in better than ten minutes; there would not be many citizens within, and that was a blessing. I could visualize what was taking place at the moment: the balding man and the electrician with drawn guns, one holding employees and citizens at bay, the other scooping money into the valise; then, if nothing goes wrong, the order to lie down on the floor, and the exit. If nothing goes wrong . . .

The palms of my hands were hot and slick with sweat, and I gripped the edge of the booth table with unconscious pressure, my nose inches from the glass like a kid looking through the window of a candy store. I seemed to be hearing the tick of a clock, even though there was no clock in the room that I could see, and the ticks were painfully slow. A man and a woman strolled by the newsstand, arm in arm, and two cars passed and a kid came by on his bicycle; the shadows cast by the buildings had begun to lengthen, encroaching on the golden wash of sunlight. The shades in the bank stayed down and the door stayed closed, but there did not seem to be anything unpredictable or volatile happening down there.

Another minute passed, and two and three—and then the bank door opened inward. I stopped breathing; but it was all right. They came out, the balding guy and the electrician, the latter an average-looking type with red hair; they came out walking, not running, closing the door behind them and then starting up the street at an even pace. The balding guy was wearing his sunglasses and carrying the valise. They watched the street ahead of them and occasionally behind them as they walked and did not see anything that bothered them and kept on coming.

When they reached the alley they turned in without hesitation because there was no one abreast of it or approaching it in either direction, on either side of the street. The balding man had his sunglasses off and his hat off before they had taken three steps into the deserted passage. I saw him shoving those items, and something from his coat pocket that would be a gun, into the valise; the other guy tugged at his scalp and the red hair came off and went into the bag, revealing him to be dark-haired, and he shoved what was probably a second gun in there as well. All of that took maybe fifteen seconds, and now they were at the alley door to the newsstand. The balding guy reached out, caught the knob, looked back, saw that the alley was still deserted and that there was no one visible on the street, opened the door, tossed the valise inside, closed the door, and with the other guy took half a dozen steps toward Pine Street.

And the trap sprung.

It happened very quickly, and I found out later that Quartermain had had a man upstairs in the attic of the Old Bavarian Inn, equipped with a walkie-talkie and giving forth with a running commentary that let the others know exactly when the valise had been dumped and the two men were unarmed in the empty alley. Two plainclothesmen came out of the malt shop next to the newsstand and another one came out of the curio store that bordered the other side of the alley and Quartermain and Favor appeared from somewhere on my side of the street, running across; the five of them converged on the alley mouth, guns drawn, and I could see another team of officers sealing off the Pine Street mouth. The balding guy and the other one had no chance to fight and no place to run; they had gun muzzles in their bellies and handcuffs on their wrists within seconds. Quartermain and Favor had taken the newsstand, jerking open the alley door, rushing inside; they came out with the valise and with the tall guy, hands shackled behind his back, just as one of the local black-and-white cruisers was pulling into the passage-way from Pine Street.

I let go of the table edge and sat back limply and said "Oh Christ!" aloud with soft reverence.

It had been just that kind of happening.

Twenty

I went to City Hall again. By previous agreement the prisoners had been taken immediately to the larger jail and police facilities in neighboring Monterey, and a trip over there would have been pointless for me; there was no way I would be allowed to sit in on the interrogation of the holdup men—and I was in no physical condition or frame of mind to deal with reporters. I also did not trust myself to make the drive, as short as it was; the few blocks to City Hall were torturous enough.

Donovan had long since gone off duty and there was a sergeant named Cole, whom I had met earlier, behind the front desk when I came in. I asked him if he had any identification on the three bank robbers, and he said yes, word had just come in: they were Androvitch and Collins and Sarkelian. That was all the information he had at the moment; he did not know which was the balding man. I thanked him and asked him if I could go into the Chief's office to await Quartermain's return, and he passed me through immediately.

When I got down there and opened the door into the ante-room, I saw that someone else was waiting for Quartermain. Robin Lomax sat primly in one of three upholstered chairs across from the secretary's desk—hands folded in her lap, knees together, back rigid—still wearing the white sleeveless dress of the morning, still looking fresh and innocent and tawny-gold healthy. But her eyes were different now; the fear was gone, leaving them old and defeated like ancient, intelligent entities forever trapped in the body of a mannequin.

The eyes moved up and over me as I entered, touching me with dull hatred, and her unpainted mouth betrayed her distaste at my appearance. Dirty old man. Gaunt-eyed and stubble-cheeked, wearing soiled clothes, smelling sour. Dirty old private detective. Subhuman species. Trash. Something odorous, something unclean: a four-letter word. The quirk of her mouth told me all that, and the old and defeated eyes confirmed it, and I felt a sudden and unreasoning anger take hold of me. What gives you the right to disparage me, lady? I thought. What gives you the right to hate me without knowing me or what I am or what I stand for? I'm no threat to you or to your shallow little existence; I'm no threat to anybody, I'm just a tired, half-assed do-gooder living in a world I never made . . .

And then I thought: The hell with it, the hell with it, she wouldn't understand and you can't take it out on her, she's hurting in her own way too. The anger faded into mild irritation and then into nothing at all. I closed the door and walked over toward her and said, "Hello, Mrs. Lomax."

"Hello," cold and remote.

"Have you been waiting long?"

"A few minutes."

"The Chief might not be back for some time."

"So I've been told."

"Is there something I can do?"

"You've done quite enough, thank you."

Yeah, I thought. I said, "All right, Mrs. Lomax," and turned and went over to the secretary's desk. He had been sitting there watching and waiting patiently. We exchanged nods, and I asked, "Is it okay if I go into the Chief's office to wait?"

He knew me well enough by now, but he was still hesitant. "Well, I don't know . . ."

"All I'm after is that couch in there. I've been up for going on thirty-six hours and if I don't get a place to lie down pretty soon I'm going to fall flat on my face. I'm not kidding you."

He saw the truth of that in my eyes, and it made up his mind for him. "I guess it's all right, then," he said.

"Thanks."

I looked at Robin Lomax again, but as far as she was concerned I was no longer there. I went into Quartermain's office and shut the door and moved directly to the old leather couch and stretched out supine with my head on one of the rounded arms. The leather was soft and cool beneath my enervated body, and I closed my eyes and put one arm across them to shut out additional light.

Thoughts—questions—began to tumble fretfully across the surface of my mind. How was Quartermain making out in the interrogation of Androvitch and Collins and Sarkelian? Had one of them killed Paige and Winestock? The balding man? Would he confess to it if he had? And Robin Lomax—why was she here? What had made her come down to sit and wait for what might be hours? Why did she want to talk to Quartermain? Why was the fear gone from her eyes, to be replaced by tired resignation? Where was her husband? And on and on and on.

I concentrated, finally, on blanking them out; they were questions that could have no answers until Quartermain returned from Monterey. One by one, they faded until they were all gone—and immediately, perversely, something else began tugging at my mind, a thought that was not a thought, an evanescent scrap, something very important, a sentence or two sentences that someone had spoken today or last night. I reached for it mentally, but a kind of warm fog seemed to be unfolding inside my head and my consciousness commenced sinking into it and I could not quite grasp the thought even though I kept on reaching and reaching and reaching . . .

Someone began gently shaking my shoulder, and I came up out of fevered and fitful darkness with a groggy sense of disorientation at first and then with returning awareness. Pain went to work in my temples in a dull, steady cadence, and harshly in my throat as I tried to swallow. I forced myself into a sitting position and pried my eyes open. Light burned at my retinas, and then diminished, and I could see all right.

Quartermain gave me a pallid smile and said, "Sorry to wake you, but I thought you'd want to talk. And I had some coffee and sandwiches made up; we both need a little nourishment."

"It's okay, Ned, thanks."

"Did you get much sleep?"

"I don't know, what time is it?"

"Quarter of seven."

"Christ, that late? I guess about three hours, but it feels more like three minutes."

I put my head in my hands and tried to gather enough strength to get up on my feet. My mouth felt cottony, and my head and throat kept on hurting. I took several thick breaths and heaved up and moved shakily over to the desk and sat down again in one of the armchairs. I was fully awake now, and I remembered the evanescent thought I had been trying to grasp just before falling asleep; but the thought itself seemed to be gone for the time being, vanished into my subconscious.

Quartermain walked around behind the desk and sank into his chair. His long face was so deeply lined that the creases looked like knife cuts, and his eyes seemed to be bleeding. I said, "You've got to get some sleep yourself pretty soon. You look dead on your tail, Ned."

"Don't I know it?" He poured coffee for both of us and slid

194

one of the cups over to me. "But Christ knows when I'll get to bed now, or when any of us will."

"Problems?"

"Yeah. Paige's death. The bald guy—his name is Sarkelian, Edward Sarkelian—claims he didn't have anything to do with the stabbing of Paige. The other two, Androvitch and Collins, claim the same thing."

"They couldn't be lying?"

"No reason for them to lie, not now. We've got them cold on the Winestock killing. One of the guns stuffed into the valise with the bank's money was the murder weapon; a ballistics check proved that. Androvitch, the tall one that waited in the newsstand, says it's Sarkelian's gun. He also says Sarkelian shot Winestock; he's trying to cop a plea."

"What does Sarkelian say?"

"He admitted it. In the face of the evidence, the public defender we got for them advised him to tell it straight, and he told it. I think you and I both figured him for a sharpie, but he's not smart at all—a strong-arm body, a three-time loser, and all for armed robbery. He knows he's going back for life anyway, with this fall, and the way things are in California these days, he knows the odds are good he'll never be executed for murder even if he's given the death sentence in court. But he flatly denies killing Paige. He says he had no motive, and the other two back him up."

I began to think about all the undercurrents that had manifested themselves in the past two days, and the kind of man Paige had been, and I was not surprised that it had turned out this way. I said, "So it's two separate murders, two separate cases."

"Some irony, isn't it? Paige's death led us to the book and the book led us to the robbery, but that's as far as it goes. The damned book didn't have anything to do with the murder of Paige, after all."

I drank a little coffee and took a bite out of a sandwich and managed to force it down. Hunger pangs instantly began to form under my breastbone. I ate more of the sandwich, mincingly. "What else did you get out of Sarkelian and the other two? Was Paige the mastermind behind the robbery?"

Quartermain nodded. "It's pretty much the way we figured. Paige met Sarkelian in San Quentin, and they struck up an acquaintance; Sarkelian was serving a ten-year stretch for a San Diego holdup. They talked about working a job together when they were on the outside again, since they were due to be released at about the same time, Sarkelian three months before Paige—some pair of incorrigibles, all right. But they didn't have anything definite in mind. It was only after Paige got out, and his parole officer found him a job in San Francisco, that Dancer's book came into it.

"According to what Sarkelian says, Paige was living in a hotel near the Tenderloin and the clerk there had a box of old paperback books that he kept around for the tenants. Paige happened to notice one of the tenants reading *The Dead and the Dying*, and recognized Dancer's name, and got hold of the book for the hell of it. He wasn't much of a reader, as his wife confirmed, but he read the thing anyway—fate, maybe, sowing the seeds of his own destruction.

"Anyway, the robbery blueprint intrigued him enough to keep the book around, but not enough for him to do anything about it at that time; he was looking for something better, something less complicated. Meanwhile, he met Judith and talked her into marrying him when he couldn't get at her any other way and moved to Glen Park. When nothing else came up, he began thinking again about the robbery Dancer had outlined and finally got in touch with Sarkelian; the two of them met and talked it over and decided it was worth looking into. So Paige contacted Brad Winestock."

"Why Winestock?" I asked.

"The two of them knew one another a hell of a lot better six years ago than Winestock's sister or anyone else thought. Paige talked Winestock at that time into helping him pull off a three- or four-thousand-dollar burglary in Seaside, and then kept most of the money for himself. It was the only job the two of them did together; Paige's leaving of Cypress Bay, for what he thought were greener pastures down south, took place just afterward."

"Paige had a way with everybody, didn't he?" I said sourly, and tried not to think of Beverly Winestock.

"Some sweet son of a bitch, all right," Quartermain said. "Well, he talked Winestock into checking out the local banks as unobtrusively as possible; when Winestock reported on the National Exchange Bank, it began to look pretty good to Paige. The fact that there were no vacant stores bordering on through alleys in the vicinity stopped them for a time, but Winestock did some more checking and found out about the old guy who ran the newsstand and how shaky things were for him. Acting on Paige's orders, he broke into the place on two separate occasions and vandalized it; inside two months the old guy was out of business."

"And Paige was *in* business."

"Yeah. He came down to Cypress Bay himself and contacted Keith Tarrant about renting the newsstand; he might have been smarter to keep his name out of it entirely, but he didn't and Tarrant turned him down. It didn't matter much; Paige got Androvitch to pose as an L.A. businessman and two days later Tarrant rented Androvitch the newsstand. All they needed then was a time when the bank would be at its heaviest with cash, and they settled on today.

"The holdup was to work exactly as Dancer had outlined it in the book, except that they figured to use Winestock as a safety valve; he was to be waiting in a car at the Pine Street mouth of the alley, in case anything went wrong, and for that and for the other errands he'd done he was in for a full fifth.

Paige would be the one to wait in the newsstand for the drop. Collins, who was once an electrician's apprentice, would handle the alarm system; and Sarkelian and Androvitch would supply the muscle. That's the way they planned it and that's the way it would have come off if Paige hadn't gotten himself killed on Saturday."

"The others must have been in a hell of a sweat when they learned of the stabbing," I said.

"They were. They couldn't figure why Paige had been killed or who had killed him; there had been no trouble among themselves, so they knew none of them had done it. And when Paige and Sarkelian met where you saw them in the park, to discuss final preparations and a time schedule, Paige didn't seem to be worried about anything. Sarkelian and the others talked it over and decided it was tough for Paige, but a four-way split was fatter than a five-way split and they didn't see any reason for not going through with the holdup as planned."

"And then I began asking questions about *The Dead and the Dying*, and about Sarkelian."

"Uh-huh. Beverly Winestock told her brother about your visit to her yesterday, and he told Sarkelian, and the cheese really began to get binding. If you or I read that book, the whole thing was blown. But they knew we hadn't read it yet; you wouldn't have been asking the questions you were asking. And when you and I went to see Winestock last night, they knew we still hadn't read it or we wouldn't have still been fishing; but they also knew, from Winestock's phone call to Sarkelian after we left, that we were dangerously close to the truth. Sarkelian ordered Winestock to meet him later at his motel in Monterey, and then went to the Beachwood—he knew you were staying there from the radio reports—on the gamble you'd have the book in your cottage rather than on your person, or that you hadn't already given it back to me. He won that hand, even though it set him up to lose the game. Then he drove down to

Dancer's, threw Paige's copy of the book into the sea, and set fire to the shack after picking the porch-door lock. If Dancer had been there, he would have died in the blaze, all right."

"How come they went through with the robbery with Dancer still alive?"

"Paige had told Sarkelian a little about Dancer, how he'd turned out millions of words in his career and how he didn't think Dancer would remember the book after twenty years. And they figured, since the book was that old, we wouldn't be able to dig up another copy in time to prevent the robbery. Like I said, Paige was the brains behind this whole thing, and Sarkelian and the other two nothing but strong-arms. All they could think about was the money. Like moths to a flame."

"How much was in the valise? How much would they have gotten away with if it had worked out the way they planned?"

"A little better than seventy thousand."

"Not much for all the trouble they went to," I said. "And for murder besides."

"Not much at all."

"Why *did* Sarkelian kill Winestock?"

"Winestock was scared, ready to crack from the pressure we put on him last night at his house; he'd been nervous as hell from the time he talked to Sarkelian in the afternoon, when you saw them together, and the liquor he'd drunk hadn't helped any. He wanted out, all the way out; he was planning to skip town, like a damned fool, and he tried to threaten some money out of Sarkelian. Sarkelian wrapped his gun in bathroom towels to muffle the noise and shot him. It was the only thing he could do, Sarkelian said. If he'd let Winestock try to make a run for it, we'd have picked him up in a matter of hours—and in his condition we'd have gotten the truth out of him sure as hell.

"After he shot Winestock, he drove the body out to Spanish Bay, with Androvitch following in their car, and left the Studebaker where it was found this morning. Spanish Bay is only about two miles from Sarkelian's motel, but even so they were damned lucky not to have been spotted in Winestock's car and stopped; if they had, it would have been finished right there."

"Except for whoever killed Paige," I said.

"Except for that."

"It's got to be the woman, Ned. Or someone connected with the woman."

"That's how it adds up," Quartermain agreed. "The same simple equation we had in the beginning."

"I take it Sarkelian doesn't know who she is."

"No. He knew Paige was bedding some local female, but he never saw the two of them together and Paige wasn't talking, characteristically. He doesn't know her name, or what she looks like. He also thinks she's the one who killed Paige."

I drank more coffee, and then asked, "Did you talk to Robin Lomax? She was waiting for you when I came in at three o'clock."

His bloodshot eyes turned grave. "Yeah, I talked to her."

"What did she have to say?"

"Some confidential information that I shouldn't discuss at all." He sighed. "But I think you've got a right to know, as long as it doesn't go any further than this office."

"You know it won't."

"All right. She'd been wrestling with her conscience and her pride all day, and she finally made up her mind to tell the real story of her relationship with Paige. Her husband doesn't know she came here today; he wouldn't like it if he did—but he's not going to know about it."

"Then that story he told us this morning *was* a lie?"

"Half lie and half truth. Robin had a fight with Jason six years ago and she had too much to drink brooding about it and she let Paige get her alone. Only he didn't try to attack her, and she didn't fight him off."

"Oh," I said, "I see."

200

"There's more to it than that," Quartermain said. His voice contained the kind of sadness a sensitive and moral man feels when he's given knowledge of the dark transgressions of people he's always liked and respected. "Jason Lomax is sterile; he's been sterile all his life."

I winced a little, involuntarily, and I thought: So Tommy Lomax is Walter Paige's son. But I did not say it. There was no point in saying it.

Quartermain sighed again. "That's why they immediately became nervous and frightened when you went to see them yesterday and mentioned Paige and told them you were a private investigator. They've both subconsciously accepted that phony fictional image of a private detective as a potential blackmailer; they thought you'd found out their secret, perhaps from Paige, and had come to shake them down. Then you confused hell out of them by telling them Paige was dead and bringing me into it, and your association with me; and that also gave them a brand-new apprehension: the threat of a scandal as a result of a police investigation. That's why they left in such a hurry last night; they wanted the opportunity to concoct a lie to cover up—expecting me to show up immediately after you left, you see. Lomax convinced Robin this was their only choice, and manufactured the attempted-rape business. I guess I don't blame him, in a way; he was only trying to protect his wife's reputation, and his own. He may be something of a fool, but he's also enough of a man to have married Robin when she told him she was pregnant, and to give the boy his name."

I agreed with that—thinking: Maybe I was a little hard on him after all; he's got his faults, but haven't we all? And my cop's mind added: But if he's that fiercely loyal to her, and if he hated Paige enough, and if they weren't playing tennis together Saturday afternoon as they claim, wouldn't he perhaps commit murder to maintain both his reputation and his wife's?

Quartermain said, "From the tone of the questions I asked

this morning, Robin was afraid we suspected her or her husband of killing Paige—perhaps even of murdering Brad Winestock, for some unknown reason. And if we uncovered the truth about her relationship with Paige, Jason's lie would look far more incriminating than it was. She decided to tell the truth, no matter how painful it would be, to save later embarrassment and misconceptions."

"That was the right thing to do," I said, "assuming that the confession wasn't a last-ditch effort to cover up. She's got a better motive than ever to have killed Paige, Ned."

"But not to have slept with him again, remember that."

"Unless she'd been carrying the torch all these years, in spite of the boy, and gave herself to him as a result, and then something happened to kindle a murderous hatred."

"Okay," he admitted reluctantly, "that's possible. I don't like it, but it *is* possible. Robin still says that she and Jason were together at the time of Paige's death, but that could easily enough be a lie."

"I'm not saying she's guilty, Ned; I'm only offering potentialities. It could also be that Paige *did* seduce Bianca Tarrant— six years ago or just recently—despite what her husband told us this morning; and that she was the one in his bed and who killed him for some reason. Or it could be, if Mrs. Tarrant *is* the woman, that her husband killed Paige in a jealous rage—the same way Jason Lomax could have done it if *his* wife were the woman. And it could even be that the woman is Beverly Winestock; that she was Paige's mistress previously and they resumed their affair after his return—or, more likely, that she went to him specifically to talk him out of whatever he was planning with her brother, maybe knowing about that Seaside burglary Paige talked Winestock into, and used her body for bargaining power. If so, and knowing the kind of son of a bitch Paige was, he could have used her and then laughed at her and tried to throw her out—and in blind rage, she stabbed him."

"All sound, logical possibilities," Quartermain said. "But if one is fact, how do we find it out? And there's another potential that I don't even want to think about: that the woman, the murderer or murderers, is or are totally divorced from anything that's happened in the past couple of days; one person, or two, who haven't entered into it at all thus far."

"Yeah," I said, "but somehow I don't think so. Paige's woman is Bianca Tarrant or Robin Lomax or Beverly Winestock; I've got a feeling about that, a hunch that—"

I stopped talking and frowned and put my coffee cup down. The evanescent thought, the certainly important scrap of dialogue that someone had spoken recently, began to tease my conscious mind again, searching for admittance. I concentrated on the thought and groped for it and caught it this time and held on, pulling it free and shaping it into coherence. And I had it. The hair on the back of my neck prickled and I had it.

I sat up straight in the chair. "How did he know?" I said aloud. "How did he know?"

Quartermain looked at me oddly. "What?"

"When you were talking to him earlier today, he said something about the woman Paige had in his bed just before he was killed. How did he know Paige had a woman in his bed Saturday afternoon—in his goddamn *bed*? I didn't think anything about it then because we were so damned tensed up, but I didn't tell him and you didn't tell him and you didn't release that information to the news media. How did he know?"

"Who the hell are you talking about?"

"Keith Tarrant," I said. "I'm talking about Keith Tarrant."

Twenty-one

Braced at the edge of the ravine, silhouetted against a deep purple-black dusk, the dark house appeared to have an aura of malevolence about it as we approached on Del Lobos Canyon Road—as if it were a crouching animal ready to leap across the gap to escape our impending arrival. All of that was foolish illusion, of course, a product of my tired mind and my depressive mood, but the sudden chill on the back of my neck was nonetheless very real.

We came to the unpaved connecting drive, and went down there under the shade of the walnut trees. There were no visible lights in any of the house's three tiers, but as we neared the two-car port I could see both the cream-colored Chrysler and the sleek blue Lotus parked inside. Quartermain braked to a stop at a diagonal that effectively blocked both cars, and we got out and moved around one of the dwarf cypress to the front door.

It was very quiet there, except for the soft lament of the wind and the rustle of leaves as it played through the branches of the walnut trees. The house itself was absolutely still. Quartermain pressed an inlaid pearl doorbell and there was the faint ringing of bell chimes within. But no one opened the door—then, or when he rang a second time.

The chill remained on my neck, and I tasted brassiness when I washed saliva through my dry mouth. I looked at Quartermain. "What do you think?"

"I don't know. I don't like it. The cars are here; they've got to be here, too."

"Unless they went out with somebody else. To a party, or to some kind of meeting."

"Yeah."

He rang the bell a third time, and the chimes tolled and died and the wind blew cool against my cheek and ruffled my hair in a way that made my scalp tingle unpleasantly. I said, "Do we wait in the car—or do we go in?"

"You get the feeling something may be wrong in there?"

"A little, yeah."

"Then I guess we'd better have a look."

He reached out and rotated the lucite doorknob with the tips of his fingers. It turned and the latch clicked and the door edged inward a couple of inches. He pushed it wider with his left hand, opening his coat with his right and brushing it back behind the service revolver still holstered at his side. We went into a short, dark foyer formed by a pair of low right-angle dividers that were solid wood panels to waist level, and staggered book and knick-knack shelves to the ceiling. Through gaps on the right I could see a shadowed dining area and a kitchen doorway; on the right, the short extension of what appeared to be an L-shaped living room, containing a set of wide polished-wood stairs leading down to the second tier. The main section of living room comprised most of the width of this top level, and the carpeted foyer blended into it off-center to the left. The entire rear wall was of glass, and one of the panels leading out onto the balcony had been left open; the wind came in through there and fingered the undrawn drapes on that side. The light filtering through the exposed glass was vague and dusky, but you could see the dark shapes of furniture, the dark shapes—

The chill that had been on my neck moved suddenly down between my shoulder blades, and I turned and reached behind me and fumbled along the wall beside the door and found a bank of switches. I touched one and nothing happened—the outside light—and touched another; indirect lighting came on instantly, transforming the darkness into mellow gold clarity.

Quartermain said, "Oh my God."

I moved up next to him at the juncture of foyer and living room. There were two long cherry-wood sofas set lengthwise in the middle of the room, facing one another, and Bianca Tarrant was sitting on the one furthest away from us—sitting there with her arms folded in an X-pattern across her breasts, fingers hugging her shoulders, forearms touching; her eyes were open wide and staring blankly, and she did not seem to have noticed that the lights had come on, much less that we were there. On one of the cushions beside her, in sharp blue-metal contrast to the pale whitish upholstery, was what looked to be a .32 caliber pearl-handled revolver.

Keith Tarrant was also in the room, and his eyes, too, were open wide and staring blankly—but they were eyes that would never see anything again. He lay at the foot of the nearest sofa, his head twisted against one of the cushions, and the dull reddish-brown color of his blood made an even sharper contrast against the upholstery. There was blood staining his white shirt as well, and blood on his beige slacks, and blood on his face, and blood on the rug around him. The way it looked, she had emptied the revolver at him and hit him with most if not all of the slugs.

Immediately Quartermain went to the far couch, reached down, and picked up the gun by its short barrel. Mrs. Tarrant did not move. He put the weapon into his jacket pocket and straightened up and went to Tarrant's body and knelt down; but he was only going through the motions. Features waxen, blood coagulated and dried, Tarrant had been dead for some time.

206

I just stood there, with a kind of poisonous nausea in my stomach, thinking: I could have prevented this, I could have saved Tarrant's life if I had caught his slip at the schoolhouse or if I had remembered it before going to sleep in Quartermain's office; I could have prevented this! And yet I knew I could not blame myself, not really, because the seeds had been sown long ago by Keith and Bianca Tarrant, just as Paige had sown his seeds with Dancer's book—and that destruction, in one form or another, had been inevitable.

Quartermain stood up again and glanced around the room and saw that there was a telephone on a stand near the polished-wood inner stairs. He shambled over there, his eyes sick and his mouth twisted into a thin grimace, and caught up the receiver and dialed a number. The summons: county investigators and, this time, a matron—and the crew, too, don't forget the crew, the clean-up boys, the necessary vultures who go to work when someone dies by violence. Come on out, boys and girl, the Tarrants are having a party on Del Lobos Canyon Road and you're the only others invited.

Quartermain said what had to be said and put down the handset and returned to the far sofa, stepping between where Mrs. Tarrant was sitting and a glass-topped coffee table that held two empty glasses and an empty gin bottle. He sat down next to her and touched her shoulder, shook her just a little. I thought for a moment that she was not going to come out of it, but then a tremor passed through her and her eyelids fluttered and her eyes took on a dull, vacuous awareness. But if she had been drunk when she shot her husband, she showed no signs of it now. She turned her head and looked at Quartermain without expression; he might have been a part of the furniture. Her mouth worked and she said, "I shot him, I killed him," in a voice that was steady and clear and as empty as the gin bottle.

He said, "Do you know who I am, Mrs. Tarrant? Can you understand me?"

"Yes," she said.

"Who am I?"

"Chief Quartermain."

He hesitated, and I knew why and felt some of his reluctance. It was time now for the ritual, the Miranda decision, the recitation of personal civil rights that is an absolute necessity before an individual about to be placed under arrest can be questioned in connection with a crime. *You have the right to remain silent, you have the right not to answer police questions, you have the right to know that if you do answer police questions, your answers may be used as evidence against you, you have the right to consult with an attorney before or during police questioning, you have the right to have a lawyer appointed without cost and to consult with him before and during police questioning in the event you do not have the funds with which to hire counsel yourself.* I listened to him saying that and looked at her sitting there, and the ritual was obscene—not because the Miranda decision itself was obscene or anything but perfectly just, but because with a thing like this, a drunken and irrational crime of passion, the enactment of the ritual is a cruel and bitter farce.

When he had finished, Quartermain asked her if she understood all of her rights as he had outlined them to her, and she said Yes, she understood, not really understanding, not really caring, and he asked her if she was willing to answer questions without benefit of counsel and she said Yes, yes, and uncrossed her arms and put her face in her hands and began to cry. Quartermain looked over at me, helplessly, but I had nothing for him. I moved forward a little and my eyes strayed again to Tarrant and all that blood, and I thought: So much blood and so much dying in the last few days, and now it's over, there won't be any more blood or any more dying, not here, not for a while. The undercurrents have surfaced and the rumbling has stopped and the violence has consummated itself and the web has unraveled. It's

208

over—or is it? For Walter Paige and for Brad Winestock and for Keith Tarrant, yes. But what about the others—what about Russ Dancer and Beverly Winestock and Bianca Tarrant and the Lomaxes and even Quartermain. Is it over for them, too? Is it *really* over for them?

Another tremor passed through Mrs. Tarrant, and it seemed to steady her somehow; she took her hands away from her face and sighed long and shuddering and looked at Quartermain again, waiting. Her face, sallow-white and streaked with mascara and greenish eyeshadow, was ghastly.

He asked, "Did you shoot your husband, Mrs. Tarrant?"

"Yes," she said. "I shot him. Yes."

"Why did you shoot him?"

"Because he . . . because he killed Walt."

"Walter Paige?"

"Yes."

"Are you certain of that?"

"He told me he did it. He said he did it for me, because he loved me, because he . . . loved . . ."

The words trailed off, and she began to slide her hands rigidly back and forth across her thighs; the emerald-green material of her suit pants made rhythmic rustling sounds that pulled at my nerves like the sound of chalk squealing against a blackboard. Quartermain said, with a mixture of gentleness and infinite weariness, "You were the woman with Paige Saturday afternoon? The two of you were lovers?"

"Yes. We were lovers. We were lovers six years ago and then he went away without saying anything, just went away, and I thought I would go insane with wanting him. But after a while I got over him enough so that life had some purpose again, and Keith and I . . . we were doing nicely, Keith tried, he always did try. And then Walt came back. He called me one day two months ago and said he wanted to see me again, he said he still loved me and needed me and was sorry he'd gone away, and I met him in Monterey that weekend and it was . . . oh God, it was just like it was six years ago, it was better, I loved him so! We were going away together. That wife, he didn't tell me about her, he wanted to spare me, you see, but it wouldn't have mattered, Keith didn't matter, nothing mattered but Walt.

"I began to see him regularly at the Beachwood, every Saturday, coming and going through the rear entrance and along the beach because we didn't want to take the chance of my coming in the front way and someone seeing me and recognizing me. I was always very careful when I came out again, too. It was . . . I don't know, it was even more exciting that way . . ."

"But your husband found out, in spite of your precautions."

"Yes. Yes, Keith found out. He knew about Walt and me six years ago, I had no idea he knew, I thought I had hidden it from him and I thought he was still friendly toward Walt and had no idea Walt had come back after all these years. That's why I didn't suspect Keith of Walt's murder, not at first. But then you told me today about Walt calling Keith five weeks ago, I don't know why Walt wanted to rent that store when we were going away together, and about Keith saying he didn't care for Walt, and I began thinking and thinking and suddenly I knew Keith had done it, even though you said you suspected someone else, I knew Keith was the one.

"After we came back from Monterey—he insisted we go even though I didn't want to—I started drinking and then I asked him if he had killed Walt, just like that. He denied it at first, but I kept on and on and he started drinking, too, and finally he admitted it, he told me he knew all about Walt and me and that I had been seeing Walt again because of the peculiar way I'd been acting, and he told me exactly how he had killed Walt and why he had killed him, and I . . . all at once I hated Keith, I hated him more than I've ever hated anyone or anything and I wanted him to be dead too.

"He was sitting over there on the other sofa, telling me how

210

he had lied to you this morning, how he'd claimed to have given me an ultimatum and I chose him instead of Walt, my God!—he knew about us back then, but only just before Walt left, and Keith never said a word to me, not a word . . . sitting over there telling me how he would have to be very careful to stand by that lie if you came to question us again and how lucky we were that you were so involved with Russ Dancer's book when it had nothing to do with his having killed Walt. He was very calm and oh so rational, talking like that with Walt's blood on his hands, and I couldn't stand it, I just couldn't stand it. Something seemed to snap inside me and I got up and went downstairs to Keith's study and got his gun and came up here and shot him while he was sitting there. I shot him and shot him and watched him die and I wasn't sorry but I . . . I don't know . . . I don't know . . ."

She stopped talking again, but her hands continued their nervous rubbing movement on her pant legs. There was moistness in her eyes once more, and she seemed to be trembling—a middle-aged woman now, broken and empty and tormented by something that could never have been and by an irrational mistake that could never be rectified. But I did not think she would break down; there did not seem to be enough left in her now for a breakdown.

Quartermain asked, to get the final piece in place, "Will you tell me what happened Saturday afternoon, Mrs. Tarrant?"

She nodded convulsively, and swallowed twice, and said, "Walt called me about two o'clock, I was waiting here for his call, he always called about two o'clock, you see. After he told me which unit he was in at the Beachwood, I made an excuse to Keith, he was home that day, and drove down to Cypress Bay and parked my car on Ocean Boulevard and walked along the beach to Walt's cottage. But Keith had been drinking and he suspected where I was going, knowing but not really *knowing*—do you understand?—about Walt and me, and so he followed me to Cypress Bay and along the beach and watched me go inside with Walt. Then he went through the gate there without being seen and up to the rear glass wall and we . . . Walt hadn't closed the drapes all the way and Keith saw us, he saw us in bed and he said he went half crazy, seeing me with Walt, what we were doing, and that was when . . . when he decided to kill . . . Walt . . ."

She squeezed her eyes shut and opened them again and went on in her empty voice, "He went back to his car and got one of the company letter openers that he kept to give away to customers, and came back and waited until I left the cottage, hiding out there, and when I was gone he knocked on the glass and Walt thought . . . he thought it was me coming back for something and opened the door and Keith shoved him inside and stabbed him before he could cry out . . . stabbed him . . . and Walt's blood was on his hands and he went into the bathroom to wash it off, and saw the glass I had used when Walt and I had a drink and put that into his pocket because it had my lipstick on it, and then he emptied the ashtray I had used into the toilet, and the whole time he was doing those things Walt was lying on the floor, dying, but Keith said he thought Walt was dead already or he would have finished the job . . . he would have finished . . ."

Her shoulders began to tremble violently and her body jerked as if she were undergoing convulsions. The tears began to flow, thick and glistening, further mingling with the mascara and the eyeshadow to stain her cheeks in grotesque, tragic-clown colors; she knuckled her eyes in a pathetic little-girl gesture and then took her hands down and pressed them hard against her stomach.

"I think I'm going to be sick," she said.

"I'll take you to the bathroom," Quartermain said, and he stood up and reached out a hand to her.

I felt as if I were suffocating. I turned and went around the other couch, not looking at what was left of Keith Tarrant, and

212

stepped out through the open glass door onto the balcony. Leaning forward against the railing, breathing deeply, I thought about Judith Paige again and how I would have to talk to her and how she would react to the knowledge of what her husband had been, the evil of him and what he had precipitated in the quiet, make-believe hamlet of Cypress Bay. And when the thought became too painful, I stopped thinking at all and looked across the canyon at the dark, shimmering meadow stretching from the ravine wall toward the horizon, and at the chaparral and pine that took over and leaned up to touch the star-spattered velvet of the sky, and felt the cool breath of a spring night blowing against my face.

And shuddered, because it was filled with the smell of blood.

About the Author

BILL PRONZINI, at the age of thirty, has been writing professionally for the past seven years. His third Random House novel, *Panic!*, is currently being filmed for major release by Hal Wallis and Universal Pictures; and his most recent book, *The Vanished*, which features the protagonist of *Undercurrent*, was recently condensed in *Cosmopolitan*. He has also published some 120 short stories in widely diversified fields, several of which have been anthologized. Recently returned to the United States after more than three years in Spain and Germany, he is at present living in San Francisco with his German-born wife and several thousand books and magazines.